Angela Pemberton

The world's furniture

A Novel. Vol. 1

Angela Pemberton

The world's furniture
A Novel. Vol. 1

ISBN/EAN: 9783337273507

Printed in Europe, USA, Canada, Australia, Japan

Cover: Foto ©Andreas Hilbeck / pixelio.de

More available books at **www.hansebooks.com**

THE

WORLD'S FURNITURE.

A NOVEL.

" Man's love is of man's life a thing apart ;
'Tis woman's whole existence......"

BYRON.

IN THREE VOLUMES.

VOL. I.

LONDON:

CHARLES J. SKEET, PUBLISHER,

10, KING WILLIAM STREET,

CHARING CROSS.

1861.

WORLD'S FURNITURE.

CHAPTER I.

CALAIS! the very name calls forth thousands of recollections to almost every Englishman, the generality of ideas are connected with Custom-House officers, and passport officials, sea-sickness and every other conceivable misery. A woman will think more of what her property has to go through than herself—her boxes turned upside down, and then inside out, locks

VOL. I.   B

broken, cords lost, addresses torn, so that no one can make out whose is whose, and all this through the greatest noise of human voices it is possible to be made, nothing can come up to a Frenchman's talk when he is excited, and whoever saw a calm one!

But we have nothing to do with all this, Calais *now*, and Calais *then*, in the days of which I am about to speak is very different. There was the same noise and apparent excitement then, but the place was different, the people were diffe-rent, and the cause of the people going there was different. I must take you back to the winter of 1828, when Calais was a haven of refuge to so many broken down, broken hearted, ruined English. A few miserable, intensely miserable hours, and they were saved from the disgrace of the King's Bench, and were as far out of the reach of bailiffs and sheriffs' officers as if they had gone to the North Pole.

The London boat was expected, it was a cold day with a bleak wind, blowing people about without any respect to persons ; the ship was in sight, but tossing so that you could only see half of it at a time, as you stood watching its progress at the end of ·the long wooden *jetée*, the chief walk then of Calais. Amongst the lookers on stood the English Consul, evidently expecting ·some one. Some thought it must be a great person for the Consul to bring himself out of his comfortable little house on the ramparts, to be knocked and blown about as he was on such a day ; but people were too cold and cross, for if you are cold you *must* be cross, to trouble themselves very much, besides it began to snow a little, it was more like sleet than snow, but it cut against the faces of the now small group, that were obliged to remain, for the mere gazers from curiosity fled, as soon as they found that there was really nothing to reward them for their trouble.

The Consul, however, remained, and buttoning up his coat as closely as he could, pulling the sleeves as low down over his hands as possible, with a very determined clap on the top of his hat, to render it still firmer, he quietly stood leaning against one of the thick stout wooden posts, till the winds and waves allowed the boat to enter. His patience was not tried long, for she appeared to come so suddenly and so quickly, that it seemed incredible the speck so lately seen in the far distance should now be entering, looking a litttle more sober between the two pier-heads.

The deck presented a sorry picture, rich and poor had evidently fared alike since leaving the opposite coast, all were sick, all were very wet, and as uncomfortable as human beings well could be—God does equalize his creatures in some things, sea-sickness is one. The moment the ship had reached the pier-head, the Consul, with the little crowd gathered near him, went as quickly as a sleet storm, which it had now increased to, drifting in their faces would permit, to the part of the harbour where she would land her passengers. All seemed anxious to be the first to land, and therefore they were twice the time accomplishing it, than if they had stood still till those before had moved on; so it is always, we try to attain that which is most difficult to be had, and generally find, if we succeed at all, we should probably have done so sooner, by allowing things to take their natural course, and saved ourselves besides an infinity of trouble.

So apparently thought one of the pas-sengers, evidently an English gentleman and an English clergyman, he was leaning with his elbow resting on the sort of cover that heads the entrance down to the fore-cabins; he was very tall and pale, and looked as if he had suffered somewhat more than the inconveniences arising from a voyage during a rough sea. He was watching a lady as she ascended the cabin steps, and said to her, " Poor Rose, how you must have suffered, and you at the best such a wretched sailor; where are the boys?"

There was no need of an answer, for they were there, behind their mother to answer for themselves, appearing none the worse for the tossing they had undergone. They were now on deck.

"Wait till all these people who seem in such a very great hurry are landed, and then we can go much more comfortably, and more safely, for those steps do not look the easiest things to mount for the children," again said the pale stranger.

"If you will take Frank, I will take Arthur," rejoined the lady, who then gave her hand to the eldest child, a beautiful boy, about five years old, and the gentleman, though apparently not over strong, lifted the other little fellow, who could not have been more than three, in his arms, and so stood ready to land when, as he said, the other passengers who were pushing forward, were on shore. Their turn soon came, and as the gentleman lifted his boy out of his arms upon the ground, the Consul came up to him, and bowing, said,

"I believe I see Mr. Chichester; I am the British Consul, Mr. Western, and understanding from our mutual friend, Bingham, you would come by this boat, I hastened down to welcome you and Mrs. Chichester."

After the usual civilities had been gone through, Mr. Western added,

"I think if we send Mrs. Chichester and your boys to my house, she will be spared a great deal of confusion and waiting, and you and I can see to all the luggage being passed, which I don't think we shall have much trouble with ; still they will, and, I suppose, must go through a certain form, and we cannot help ourselves, and must submit."

After sundry exclamations and explanations, first on the part of one of the Custom House officers, on seeing a lady with two children quietly getting into a carriage without going through the passport office, and then Mr. Western trying to explain very politely that all was quite right, they rolled off in the thing on wheels we had the courtesy just now to term a carriage. It was, however, as unlike one as anything meant to be drawn by a horse could be: it was more like a blue bottle cut in half, and put on two wheels. It rattled over the stones, crossed the drawbridge leading into the town, went on through the market-place, passing the town-hall, a fine old building with the telegraph at the top, which looked, when working, something between an acrobat out of place, and one of those children's toys in the shape of a harlequin, that, on pulling a little string, all the arms and legs move about, for there were no telegraphic wires in those days.

The conveyance continued its course down the Rue Royale, and finally, on turning to the left, drew up at a small-looking white house, where Mrs. Chichestsr and her boys got out; she, inwardly grateful they had arrived without any broken bones.

It was a pleasant little house inside, and an English servant opened the door. It looked cheering to see an English face. How we yearn after anything from our own country when we are absent, even if we have but just left it! And so felt poor Mrs. Chichester; the " Good evening, ma'am," sounding more cordial in her ears than it had ever done before.

They were taken into a pretty sitting-room, looking on to the ramparts; indeed, had the windows been low enough, you could have walked out on to them. A bright fire was burning, and, altogether, there was an air of bachelor comfort in the room that made it homely; everything was so very untidy, a writing-table covered with everything useful and useless; pipes and a snuff-box—for Mr. Western was not a young man, and, therefore, thought snuff was allowable—walking-sticks of all sizes and shapes, a gun, and lying on the rug before the fire, was a dog, a large white and liver-coloured setter, evidently accustomed to have particular care taken of him; he lifted his head on the entrance of the strangers, and slowly getting up, walked up to them with his tail down, and with his nasal organs ascertained whether he had to meet friends or foes.

Little Frank shrunk up close to his mother. "Oh, mamma, the big dog will bite," he said, in a questioning tone.

"Don't be such a stupid little coward, Frank," said Arthur, "look here, I am not afraid."

However, the dog appeared not to care much for Master Arthur's advances, for he walked away, but turned round and looked at Frank, and gave a scarcely perceptible wag with his fine, feathery-looking tail. The boy saw it, and seemed to feel as if a sudden understanding had arisen, that the dog meant to re-assure him that he would not hurt *him*.

Mrs. Chichester sat down in a large leather arm-chair, threw her head back, and closed her eyes; she looked ill and unhappy. Frank came and sat on a stool at her feet, and watched the fire and the dog; he did not feel afraid after that gentle wag. Arthur climbed up on the window-seat, and watched the snow falling piece by piece, till it melted away on the ground. There was not a word spoken till about half-an-hour had passed, and the street-door was heard to open, and footsteps coming towards the room they were in. Little Frank's face brightened up.

" There's papa, I'm so glad !"

"So am I," said Arthur, "for I hope we shall get some tea now."

"Poor papa must be so tired," was the only rejoinder Frank made.

They were at the door now, and walked in.

"What a room to have brought you into, Mrs. Chichester, I am quite ashamed of it," exclaimed Mr. Western, "but I suppose Mrs. Jones thought it was the warmest; and Don, too, here. Get up, you great big fellow, why you take up the whole fire."

Don slowly rose, stretched himself, then shook himself, and appeared afterwards perfectly awake, and to begin to understand that he had to do with visitors.

"Indeed, I think you have no cause to apologize either for the room or the dog, Mr. Western, but we will release you now if you will tell me where our lodgings are you kindly secured, I think you told Bingham they were near to your house," said Mr. Chichester.

"Indeed I shall not allow one of you to stir till you have had some refreshment, there can be nothing ready for you in your own rooms, and you must be nearly famished."

"I am," said Arthur.

"Well, my boy, what will you have?"

"Oh, anything, thank you, only I am very hungry."

"Mrs. Chichester, tell me if you would not prefer some tea to anything else, I know ladies are generally great tea drinkers."

"I should," said Mrs. Chichester, "but really it seems troubling you so, such a host of us, and I have no doubt we should manage to get something at our lodgings if you will let us go."

"Indeed I will not," said Mr. Western, and ringing the bell, Mrs. Jones in her black dress and white apron appeared as if by magic. "Mrs. Jones," began Mr. Western in rather a humble tone, "will you be so kind as to get tea ready in the dining-room, and anything cold you may have, and if you please to have a good fire—" Mr. Western seemed to get more and more humble. What cowards men are with women! and especially a bachelor with his house-keeper, if he puts her out a little, it is so easy for her to put him out a great deal, he does not know how to find fault, he dare not, and she knows it. They are worse than wives, for a man can bully his wife, but he dare not his housekeeper. I daresay Mr. Western will suffer for his entertaining a gentleman and lady and two children without permission. However, we will leave him in happy ignorance of what may be in store for him, stuffing the boys with cakes and sweetmeats, and urging Mr. and Mrs. Chichester to eat much more than it was physically possible for them to accomplish.

Frank had felt a cold nose touch his

little hand as it lay on his knee, which made him start; he was a timid child, but a pair of large brown eyes with a gentle expression looking into his face, made him without fear pat Don's head, and offer him some of his good things, and so they established a firm friendship.

We will leave them now thus comfortably engaged, and go back a few years, to learn a little of the Chichesters before they came to Calais.

CHAPTER II.

Rose Fordyce was the only daughter of Sir John Fordyce, a wealthy proud Scotchman, her mother died when she was but a few weeks old, leaving her and an only boy about six or seven years of age to be brought up by a man she knew to be without heart and very little principle. She trusted, however, her son William would be a kind protector to his sister at the age she would most require it. Sir John lived at Burwood, in Leicestershire, the entire year, and, since his wife's death, he was a thorough country gentleman, fonder of his horses, dogs, and gun than he was of his children.

As his little daughter became old enough, he had a first-rate governess for her, and William was sent to Eton; so the brother and sister met but two or three times a year, till she was about fifteen. There was, however, a constant correspondence kept up, so that their affection for each other was not diminished. Then William came home for a year previous to his entering Oxford. It was a very happy year to Rose, they were always together, and, as happy times generally do, it passed very rapidly. Before leaving for Oxford, William told his father he thought, as his sister was now sixteen, it was time to think of his opening his house a little, and entertaining his county neighbours. It was then arranged they were to commence their first gaieties at Easter.

Easter came, and with it brought William, and with him Mr. Chichester, a young man whose acquaintance he had made at Oxford, and who had just been ordained. George Chichester was a young man of good family, but no property, as fascinating as he was poor, but a high-minded, upright, generous fellow, every one liked George, and no one in any difficulty could get out of it, unless George was there to help them.

At this time, Rose Fordyce was between sixteen and seventeen, she had never seen anyone at her father's house but those of her father's type, coarse in words, and thoughts, and very often appearance, men who were not fit to come into the drawing-room after dinner, who had no inclination for it, far preferring smoking and drinking with each other; they looked on women as necessary evils, but that they need not be annoyed with when they were tired and sleepy.   It was therefore by no means surprising that Rose thought Mr. Chichester something totally distinct from mankind; she was very pretty, but nothing more, she was neither short nor tall, very black curling hair, a clear but dark complexion, with rosy lips, and rosy cheeks. George Chichester thought nothing about her, beyond her being William's sister, but he could not fail to see that she admired him, but he did not feel much surprised when he was introduced to the principle people that formed her society. He began to pity her, and thought it very sad she should be thrown amongst such a set of rough uncouth creatures; but after all she was little more than a child, so perhaps it might not matter, and so he thought no more about it. He remained Sir John's guest for a week, and had to leave to perform his duties as curate at a little village in Essex, on the borders of Epping Forest.

So time went on, and two years had elapsed. William was spending his last term at Oxford, but it was nearly over, and he was anxiously expected at Burwood by his father and sister. His father was proud of him because he was his heir, Rose was fond of him because he seemed to understand her, and was always kind to her. He wrote a few days before his return, saying, " My old friend, Chichester, has promised to come with me. I hope you have not forgotten him."

Rose's heart jumped about in a most ungovernable manner, she thought she was never so pleased with the idea of William before, and the days seemed to pass very slowly. But when the day arrived, and they too, all her anticipated pleasure had fled, she even got out of the way, and had to be called and hunted for at least a quarter of an hour before she could be found. " Why, Rose, you look as if you had met a ghost, where are all your roses gone to?" her brother exclaimed. They soon appeared, and she became as crimson as she was before pale. She shook hands with George without looking at him, but he saw all, and felt all; and felt she must have loved him very deeply for two years to have made no change, or if any, to have increased the feelings of almost a child into those of a woman. He thought her wonderfully improved, and he could not imagine how it happened that though he had not given a thought about meeting her, now she was there, his heart was beating, and he could not find one word to say for himself.

It did not take many days before George and Rose perfectly understood each other; but George held nothing but the miserable pay of a curate, Rose's fortune depended entirely on what her father chose to allow her, with the exception of one hundred a year that she had from her mother's fortune. She thought of course her father would be very liberal, and William would be so glad for her to marry his old chum. George thought a little differently, but neither liking to endure suspense, it was arranged William should be consulted first, and then Sir John's consent to their marriage asked at once.

Rose went to her room after their decision very happy, and full of bright hopes; George went at once, and, in his open-hearted manly way, told William his tale, and asked him for his aid with Sir John, as he naturally expected opposition. Such a conclusion to affairs had never for a moment suggested itself to William, and he was taken by surprise completely; he was vexed with George for falling in love with his sister, because he liked him, but did not like Rose marrying a man without rank or fortune, and he was vexed with Rose for being such a little fool.

George instantly saw he should have as much difficulty, if not more, with the brother, as with the father; but it could not be helped, matters had gone too far to retreat;

he would not if he could, for Rose had become very dear to him. So he said, " I am afraid, Fordyce, the affair is against your wishes, and that I need not look to you to plead my cause with Sir John."

" There is no use, Chichester, in my trying to make you believe I am pleased, I am not, for to speak plainly, it is a miserable prospect for Rose; but I won't oppose you with my father, though I cannot help, so I shall leave you to say what you like to him, I will speak to Rose."

Poor George felt very uncomfortable, he was young, and had never thought of marrying; and even now had never taken into consideration the expenses that, as a married man, would be entailed on him. He had not had time in fact, the whole thing seemed so sudden, so unexpected, but there was nothing for it now but to summon up all the courage he could, and face the proud baronet; try what best might be done with poverty, honour and truth, against pride, wealth and ambition.

He found Sir John very busily engaged, at least having the appearance of being so, in the library, which he always looked on as his own especial room.

"Oh, are you looking for William, Chichester?" said Sir John, as George opened the door, "he is, I think, in the stables, looking at the new mare I bought for Rose yesterday."

"No, Sir John, I have just left William, I came here to ask you to give me a few minutes' conversation."

George began to feel a little in want of words to express all he had to say, so he waited a moment; and Sir John telling him to take the arm-chair by the fire, and if it was anything requiring his advice, he should be most happy to tell him what he thought best. However, the condescending speech was all lost on George, who had been gathering together all his argumentative powers, which are generally tolerably strong in an Irishman, and he came out with the upshot of his visit to Sir John before he scarcely knew it himself; when once fairly launched out with his wishes, he got on very well, and argued as if Sir John had already expressed great disapprobation, whereas the worthy baronet had merely opened his small grey eyes a little wider, and had not uttered a syllable. He let George proceed for some time, and when he paused for a moment, apparently only to take breath, Sir John said,

"Mr. Chichester, I think you forget your position, and *my* position, pray do not let us waste more time in discussing such a ridiculous affair; I think, however, as you so far forgot yourself as to speak on the subject to my daughter, it would perhaps be wiser for you not to prolong your visit in my house, though I am quite certain Miss Fordyce had too much proper pride ever to have permitted you for one instant to imagine she could consider you in any other light than an acquaintance. I have far other views for my daughter; I need not add, I think, that I request you will not see her again."

George, too, was proud, but his pride was of a different sort of stuff from Sir John's; he got up, bowed, and left the room. He was deeply hurt, he had scarcely been treated like a gentleman; he would leave the house, and none of them should hear of him again. He walked into the garden, it led down, the farther end of it, across a kind of fenced in field to a little wood. He went in that direction, he wanted to think for a few minutes, for after all, Rose was the daughter of the man who had, as he thought, so insulted him, and he must bear something for her sake; but he had borne more than most men would, almost more than he himself could. But there was little time for him to think, for the moment he entered the

wood, he heard footsteps, and instantly afterwards William and Rose appeared. She had
the remains of tears very visible, but she
looked tolerably happy, and a bright smile
came over her face on seeing George, it was
soon to be overclouded; but that smile made
George a different man, he determined to
brave all for her; he would not break her
heart, whatever her father and brother chose
to do. So he asked William to allow him
half an hour with Rose, and if then he would
join them. William, who had been softened
a little by Rose's appealing ways, and being
really very fond of George, was wavering
between her prospect of happiness as his
wife, or as the wife of one of their county
hunting, drinking squires.

So William left them, and George then
told Rose all that had just passed between
her father and himself; he could not remain
that was certain; but what was to be done?
They thought of so many plans, William

would not help them, though he promised to do nothing to aggravate the mêlée. At last George determined to go to a village three miles from Burwood, where he could remain during the next fortnight, see and hear from Rose, and know how all was going on. He had but a fortnight's more leave, so everything had to be concluded during the time; but they thought a fortnight quite enough for all their plans to be settled, and so indeed it proved.

William went into his father when he left George and Rose, and heard what had passed; his father was in a great fury, and threw half the blame on William for bringing him to Burwood. This did not improve Sir John's cause, for William was annoyed at his unjust accusations, and went out at the end of a very long half hour to join his sister, much more inclined to aid them then he was before.

" My father is much annoyed, Chichester, but it can't be helped, and will blow over;

there may be happy days for you and Rose yet."

They all went in, and that afternoon George left. Ten days afterwards and Rose was gone too, and when they heard from her, she had become George Chichester's wife, determined to cling to him rich or poor. William was a little annoyed at first, but not so much so, as if his father had been less violent. Sir John swore he would never see her again, and would not leave her one shilling; and he kept his word, he died some four years later, leaving everything to William, and had refused to receive a letter even from Rose, forbidding William also to have any communication with her of any kind.

Rose felt William's neglect of her, which she imagined voluntary, very deeply, but she never complained; she found no difficulty in putting aside all her girlish habits and ways, suiting herself to her new position of a poor curate's wife; she loved her husband devotedly, and she was quite happy. Year after year elapsing, and still no notice taken of any of her letters, she at length gave up writing, and gave up too thinking about it; and so when George came home one day, and told her that he had heard the news of Sir John's death, she felt it less than was almost natural; but then her father did not love her husband, and how could she love any one who did not love him. She expected to hear now from her brother, but no letter came, and so the whole past was nearly obliterated from her memory.

She had been married some five or six years now, and was very happy, she had two little boys, the eldest three, and the youngest just born, Arthur and Frank, whose acquaintance we have made already. It was now for the first time that troubles seemed to gather round them; the old Rector died, and the newly appointed one, let George Chichester understand he should bring his

own curate with him. This was a dreadful
state for him to find himself in. A wife and
two children, and only her £100 a year to
depend on; he now thought of the madness
of his having dragged Rose down to this
miserable position; but he must do something; he must instantly set to work and
look out for another curacy. He advertized,
he wrote scores of letters, he went to London
daily, but all to no purpose, there was nothing
to be had. Six months passed, the new
Rector and new curate had arrived, and
George with his family had to turn out of
their happy little home; they took lodgings
in London, and George hunted up a few of
his old college friends, but the friends of our
school or college days are not generally so
anxious to renew the acquaintance when they
find us poor, and in want of assistance.

There was one, however, Frank Bingham,
who had stood godfather to his youngest boy,
that cared a little whether George was rich or

poor; he had once fought a battle for him at school, and Frank had never forgotten what he owed George Chichester for that : and so he not only promised to exert himself, but did do so and finally succeeded, but as he said, very badly, for all he could get was the chaplaincy at Calais, through his old friend, Mr. Western.

But that was something. They could live there with Rose's money, and what he would get, better even than they did in Essex. But they had to wait for this, and nearly eighteen months elapsed between the promise of his obtaining it, and the time that we saw them all land in Calais; for the old clergyman who was there, did not like giving up the duty, though he was so aged that few could understand a word he said. And so he went on from month to month, and, probably, would have gone on till he died, had not Mr. Western written for Mr. Chichester to come, as, if he did not, Mr. Letheby never would give in. It was still a few weeks after George's arrival, before Mr. Letheby fairly was off.

But it is time now we should see how the Chichesters get on in their new home.

The word 'new' put before home, always gives it a chilling sound; it quite takes away the sweet recollections that are generally called forth by the word itself. And how many heart-aches there generally are in a new home !

CHAPTER III.

THE lodgings Mr. Western had secured for the new English clergyman, were in the Rue Française, a street running parallel with his own, the gate leading into the Basse Ville, forming, as it were, a separation to the two streets, which, otherwise, might have been one.

The entrance to the house was very good. You went in the great, big green-painted doors which took you into a court-yard with a little garden beyond it, and you turned to the left on entering, which led to the stairs; the rooms were on the first floor, tolerably comfortable and pretty.

But it was an old-fashioned house, and though the walls could be hidden with a few prints of Napoleon's exploits, still you could not cover the ceiling, which looked very like a barn painted, for the great, heavy wooden beams ran right across the sitting-room, and nothing could hide them. The floor was painted more in the German style than French, but there was a piece of carpet in the centre, apparently for the legs of the table to be a little bit warmer than the legs of the in-mates, for nothing but the table benefited by the arrangement. The fire-place, too, looked as if it were obstinate on one point, and that was, against having a large fire.

However, these ideas only struck the Chi-chesters on their first instalment, and they wore off with time, and all else was what they required, plenty of room, and very clean.

They had been in Calais now about six months, and all seemed going on very quietly and satisfactorily. Arthur went to a French tutor, Monsieur Renaud, daily, and was improving in every way rapidly. He was a beautiful boy; very dark, with a large quantity of black curly hair, large grey eyes— their expression was their drawback, they gave you an idea of bad temper, and his mouth, which was peculiarly small and pretty, had also the same fault; but every one noticed and petted the handsome English boy. Frank was too young and too delicate to go with his brother, and his time was chiefly devoted to Don, and Don's to him.

Mr. Western was almost their only constant visitor. He was a kind-hearted, liberal-minded man; at the time the Chichesters first arrived, he must have been about sixty years of age, his hair perfectly white, with rather a florid complexion, and a stout, strongly-built frame. He took a great fancy to little Frank, probably because he found that Don had done the same. It is astonishing how very sensitive we are about our dogs, quite as much, if not more so, than we are about our children. And Frank had paid devoted attention to Don, whereas Arthur rather treated him like a dog.

One day, Mr. Western came in after there had been a heavy shower, so that both master and dog had their feet rather muddy. Mrs. Chichester was sitting at the table writing, the two boys were together at the window; Arthur, with a book in his hand, looking very earnest, and not over-pleased, little Frank had a piece of paper, out of which he was trying very hard to cut a dog; his small, delicate fingers seemed scarcely strong enough to hold the scissors, but yet he grasped them very tightly. He raised his face up on hearing footsteps, and a bright look came over his gentle, loving face. He was like his father in disposition, affectionate and generous beyond measure.

The door opened, and in bounded Don;

Don's embraces were sometimes rather rough, and on this occasion particularly so, for he upset Frank off the stool he was sitting on, and came with his wet coat against Arthur's clean dress. Now if Arthur was more put out by one thing than another, it was in his clothes having a spot of dirt of any kind on them, it was quite a sufficient punishment for him at any time to be obliged to put on a soiled dress.

"Get away you dirty, horrid dog, look what you have done," cried Arthur, his eyes flashing, and his colour rising till his face was scarlet.

"Here, Don, come here, sir, go out and stay on the mat," said Mr. Western, opening the door, out of which Don slunk very much ashamed of himself, not exactly understanding why he was treated so.

In the meantime, Frank got up, pulled his little frock straight, pushed his curly hair off his face, laid the paper and scissors on the stool, and pushed it up into a corner of the room, and then went up to Mr. Western and said, with his eyes full of tears, making them look more loving than ever, "You don't turn me out of the room when I come and see you and have dirty shoes, but you have sent Don away;" and out he went to look after his favourite.

"What a heart that child has got," said Mr. Western, " he will never do to fight his way in the world, you must make him more selfish and less sensitive, Mrs. Chichester, or he will have many a heart ache, that my friend Arthur here will be spared. I am very sorry, my little man, Don was so demonstrative : has he made you very dirty ?"

"Oh, I think I can rub off the spots," said Arthur, who had been engaged ever since the misfortune trying to do so.

"I have come to tell you I am off for ten days to England, can I do anything for you, Mrs. Chichester ? buy any pins or needles, or tea, or any of those things that ladies won't believe to be good here?"

"No, I shall not trouble you with any commissions, but I think George wishes to send a book over," she replied, "if you will take care of it for him. But I am very sorry you are going, we shall miss you dreadfully even for so short a time; it is very selfish of me, is it not? but I don't know what George will do for his long walks, he will never go alone, and they do him so much good, though I fear he is not very strong; don't you think he looks ill?" and as she asked the question, such an anxious expression passed over her face, that had Mr. Western thought so he could not have said it, so he merely answered:

"No, indeed Chichester is looking better since he came here, I think."

His answer was true, for he did look better than the day he landed, but he was not what he was when in England. He was paler if possible, and much thinner, and he had acquired a slight stoop, which gave him the appearance of always looking weary, and as if he had not the strength to hold himself upright. George had never been a strong man, and the anxiety he had suffered for the last three years on account of his wife and children, was beginning to tell upon him.

"Do you think he will be in soon, for I should like to see him; I must go by to-night's mail, and, therefore, I have not too much time to get everything in order for me to be able to go in peace."

"I don't think he will be very long," she replied, "he was only going to see those English people that arrived last week, and that are living on the Place; I think a physician and his daughter."

"Oh, yes, I know who you mean, Dr. and Miss Davies; I have seen them walking on the pier, he seems very ill; I believe they have come over for change of air only. Have you seen them, did they call on you?"

"No, I have not; they called but I was out, I suppose I must return their visit, but I find little time for going out."

"Well, I must be off. God bless you! take care of yourself, and don't be worrying about your husband, he will get so strong this winter that you will begin and wonder how you could ever have thought him delicate. Good-bye, Arthur, what shall I bring you from England?"

"A pocket knife if you please, Mr. Western."

"Very well, so I will, only mamma will scold me if you cut your fingers; but where is my little Frank? I thought he was here."

"No," said Arthur, "he went out of the room almost directly you came."

" I must look for him, for I must

say good-bye to him, too;" and out he went.

He had not far to look, for on opening the door he saw Frank on his knees with a towel in his hand, rubbing Don all over as if he were drying a child. Don was lying on a mat in front of one of the bed-room doors, licking Frank's hand every time it came within reach of his mouth, and quite contented with his position. The performance was just drawing to a close as Mr. Western came out, and he heard Frank say, "There, Don, now you are as nice and clean as Arthur is, and you shan't be turned out of the room; do you feel comfortable, Don, dear old fellow," and he put his little face down and buried it in Don's long hair.

"Holloa, Frank what are you about? I have only just missed you. Here, I have come to say good-bye to you, for I am going away for a few days. What shall I bring you back?"

Frank, during this speech, had slipped off Don, and sat on the mat by the side of him, and put his arm round the dog's neck, who had also made a move on seeing his master, and sat upright, ready to start at the first order.

"You are going away, I am very sorry, but you will come back soon, wont you?" and he got off the floor and took hold of Mr. Western's hand, "and you wont take Don, will you?"

"Oh no, Frank, I shall leave Don to take care of Mrs. Jones, and you can call for him whenever you like for a walk."

"But you must not leave him with Mrs. Jones, she says dogs are always in the way, and no room is fit to be seen if a dog is let into it, and I know she won't give Don anything to eat, don't leave him with Mrs. Jones; I don't want you to bring me anything back, ouly let him stop here; I know papa will let me have him, oh do, dear Mr.

Western. You will stay with me, Don, wont you?" and the child put both his arms round the dog's neck, and held him very tight, for fear he should get away. "Oh, here is papa; papa you will let me have Don while Mr. Western is away, wont you? he wont be happy with Mrs. Jones. I will take such care of him, and always wipe his feet if they are muddy, you must, you must, papa."

"What is all this about?" said Mr. Chichester, who had now got within distinct hearing, "you going away, Western, and Frank taking away Mrs. Jones' character, what does it all mean?"

"Why it is simply that I have to run over to England for ten days, and I came to say good-bye to you all, and see if I can do anything for you, and Frank on hearing it, insists upon having the entire charge of Don."

"Well, come in and tell me what you are going for."

"No, I must not go in again, for I am pressed for time; but your wife tells me you have a book you want taken over, can you bring it to me this evening, and then we can have half an hour's chat before I start."

"Well, I will," said George, and Mr. Western kissed Frank, and was nearly gone, when the child again begged to have Don left with him.

"I will settle with your papa to-night, my boy, and if he wishes it, you shall have Don under your own charge."

Frank was quite satisfied, he knew his father never refused him anything, he followed him into the sitting-room, and made him promise to bring Don back at night when he went to see Mr. Western.

"How tired you look, George," said his wife, after he had sat down, and sent Frank off to his paper and scissors again, " you look worried too, what is the matter ?"

" Nothing, Rose, it is very warm out, and I walked rather faster than usual." He had that worn look about his face that often crossed it now.

" Did you see the Davies' ?"

" Yes, and they are very anxious to see you and the boys ; you must call there, Rose, as soon as you can, they seem nice friendly people."

" I will, only I have so lost the habit of paying visits, that it seems quite an under-taking now even to make one, they are living over that large shop on the Place, where they sell those pretty carved ivory things, are they not ?"

" Yes, and very good rooms they have, and it is a cheerful look out for the old gentleman, as he cannot walk a great deal."

" How you will miss Mr. Western, George, you must take Arthur to walk with you, for you must not give that up, I am sure it does you so much good."

About a week after Mr. Western had gone, Rose gave birth to a little girl, it was on the 18th of August, about a year after their arrival in Calais. It was a cause of great delight to Rose that she had a little daughter, she had always thought a daughter must be so much more to a mother than a son possibly could be. She knew when her boys grew up; they would have to leave her, and even before, for their school-days must soon begin, Arthur's had already, and though as yet he was only away during part of the day, very soon they would have to make some arrangements about sending him over to England to a boarding school. She should keep Frank at home longer, because he was a delicate child, and not able to bear the rough usuage of school boys; still his turn too must come sooner or latter; but with a girl it is so different; she need never part with her, she could teach her a great deal herself, and she could have masters at home; and it was a long, long time time to look forward to, to when she might marry; but that was not parting with her, on the contrary, she should gain a son, and not lose a daughter.

So Rose was very happy. What a merciful Providence it is that veils the future from our eyes, what one of us would, if we could, read the future. We think, perhaps, at times, we should like to know where we shall be, or what we may be doing so many months, or so many years hence; but were it really in our power, we should shrink from it, and rather live on in ignorance of what our fate may be. For we all have our trials, and we generally feel there are yet plenty in store for us; we are born to them, and women, I think, must have been born *for* them.

Mr. Western returned when Rose's baby

was a fortnight old, he had been longer absent than he wished or expected, people generally are. I never yet knew anyone leave home for a given time, that something, or some one did not interfere with the return. He had a warm welcome from all the family, Don included, who had quite become one of them; he even looked on the baby as an intrusion, and was not quite sure at first how to receive it, but Frank took him in hand, and made him pay gentle respect to his little sister.

In Catholic countries every saint has some especial day, and as that of St. Hilda happened to be on the day of the Chichester's arrival in Calais, they decided on that name for their little girl, as there was no one either Rose or George were anxious to name their little girl after; and Hilda being a pretty name, Hilda it was decided to be. Mr. Western was to be her godfather, Miss Davies her godmother, and Rose was to be the other. There was no church, so George christened her in his own drawing-room, when she was about three weeks old.

CHAPTER IV.

FOUR years have elapsed since the close of the foregoing chapter, and though great is the change that Time has produced in appearances in our little family group, yet circumstances have remained much as they were. I must try and let you see yourself the changes, and I don't think I can do so in any better way, than taking them one by one, as they are, and letting you see a little into their thoughts and feelings. George Chichester has for five years discharged the duties of British Chaplain at Calais, as few would have done, discharged them willingly, and conscientiously. You perhaps think there could be little for him to do—you are wrong, he had much to do; it is true there were few of the ordinary duties imposed on a clergyman in England, but, nevertheless, there were duties to perform that few clergymen would have done.

His chief task lay in visiting and offering such consolation as he could to the many of his countrymen that fled over there for refuge from the disgrace of imprisonment; sad were the histories he daily had to listen to, but he was never weary of well doing, and he had a kind of sympathy for these poor exiles, which he was almost unconscious of himself, that rendered him pitiful and courteous to all.

The second winter he passed in Calais told sadly on his health; the winter of 1829-1830 was one of the most bitter any of the inhabitants ever remembered. The cold was so intense that many died from exposure to it, and Mr. Chichester, who could never have been considered a strong man, felt it severely;

he had a serious attack on his chest in the January, which so reduced him, that it was months before he felt equal to any exertion. Each successive winter found him less able to bear the searching cold of the climate, and we now find him at the end of the year 1833, sadly changed from the George Chichester we first became acquainted with. He still performs the duty on Sunday, but that is all he is able to do, he can no longer take his walks with Mr. Western, nor has he done so for more than a year; he is the shadow of his former self, his stoop has increased as his strength has diminished, and a nasty hacking cough is constantly annoying him.

The change in George has not failed to work an equal change in his wife; her increasing anxiety for him has so worked upon her, that not a vestige of youth is left. It is true she has passed the years that are generally termed young, but many a woman of three-and-thirty is still very youthful; and how often are women, not married, termed "girls" when they are even nearer forty than thirty! But Rose cannot certainly be called a girl, scarcely a young woman, there are lines in her face, and a compression about the mouth, that tell of the wear she has gone through, and the restless days she has passed.

George never now goes out without her, he will take nothing but what she gives him, and he never tries to exert himself unless she urges him to do something to please her. She even writes all his sermons.

Saturday afternoon is as regularly set apart by her for writing the sermon for the next day, as it was by himself when he was first ordained. She does all cheerfully. She never regrets the day that made her his wife; she will now tend him as he before shielded her. A thought of her brother sometimes crosses her, that he might have sought some news of her, but she bears no ill-will towards him, for he used to like George, and so she

only supposes he cannot trace him.   Arthur
is now shortly expected home for his holidays; for the last two years he has been over
to an English school at Chiswick, under the
care of a clergyman, who unable to get a
living any other way, was obliged to take
pupils; he receives Arthur at rather a less
rate than his other ones, because he is a
clergyman's son, and so the Chichesters were
able to send him their boy, which otherwise
with their small means would have been impossible.

Arthur is a wonderfully handsome boy,
about eleven years old; he has not much
altered from what he was, excepting that he
is taller, the expression of his face is the
same; he is proud, rather overbearing, he
hates being told he is good looking, his disposition resembles his mother's father, more
than any one's else; he is a brave, manly
fellow, and has a proportionate contempt for
all who are not so.

Frank is the same as he was, gentle, loving, and generous beyond measure, still delicate, and unequal to cope with his brother in many of his amusements; devoted to his sister Hilda, and Don, who has now, we may say, completely become his property; but Frank is quite as tall as Arthur, so slight and fragile looking that he looks as if a breath of wind must injure him. He feels proud of his dark manly brother, and looks up to him, as if all he did must be right. Don never quite returned to his original home, after his first visit to Frank; he occasionally devoted half a day to his old master, but the new one seemed more to his taste, he gave back with interest all Frank's affection for him.

But I must not forget Hilda, for she it is, I suppose, that I must term my heroine. Hilda at this time was between four and five years old. She was a small, graceful child, not pretty, but peculiar looking; she was dark and pale, more of a Spanish complexion; her chief beauty was her eyes, and they were wonderful, they were very large, and either grey or blue, for they looked one colour at one time, and then seemed to change with the expression of her face; her hair was black, and very wavy; her nose small and straight, but her mouth it is difficult to describe, for it was like her eyes, rarely the same; her lips were red and full, and when she smiled, her whole face lighted up, it was like sunshine · after a cloud passing by, for the natural expression of her face was sombre. She was a quiet child, but had deep feeling, a slight to Frank from anyone would never have been forgotten or forgiven, she was devotedly attached to him and her father.

Mr. Chichester was sitting in an arm-chair by the fire, with little Hilda on his knee; he was leaning back with his eyes closed, and she was playing with his hair.

After tiring herself with that amusement, she sat perfectly still for a minute or two watching his face, at last she exclaimed, " Papa, your face is not tumbled like Dr. Davies, why is his face so ugly, your nice face wont look like his, will it ?"

" No, my darling, I don't think it ever will, for I shall never be old like Dr. Davies."

" I hope not, papa, for I should not like to kiss you if it were."

" Should you be very sorry, little Hilda, if I left you, never, never to see you again."

George had often thought he should not live long, but he had never before alluded to it to any one, and it seemed, after having uttered the words, to strike him more forcibly, almost as if it occurred to him the first time, and it brought with it such a train of sad forebodings, that he scarcely heard his little girl's reply. " If you go away, papa, I shall go too, do you hear ; you shan't go and leave me; when are you going, tell me, papa ?"

Thus forced to answer the child, he said, " If l go away from you, Hilda, it is because God will choose to take me; and you must stay with poor mamma, and make her as happy as you can, by being very good, and doing all she tells you, because mamma, too, will be sorry for me to leave her."

Hilda thought for a moment, she felt very much inclined to cry, but she knew it always vexed her father whenever she did, and at that moment she would rather do any-thing than that. Her large eyes were full of tears, but she kept them from falling; at length a happy thought seemed to cross her childish mind, for she smiled, and looking into her father's face, said, " I know, we will all go together, you shan't go alone; mamma, and Arthur, and Frank, and Don, and then we shall none of us want to cry, for I am sure I should if you left me."

They were here interrupted by the entrance
of Mrs. Chichester and Frank, who had been
down to the pier to meet Arthur, he was
expected by that day's boat, but it had not
come in, nor was it even in sight, and they
attributed its delay to a probable fog in the
Thames. They came in to have an early
dinner, and start off again. Little Hilda full
of what she had been talking about to her
father, was intent on telling her new plan to
her mother and Frank, but George stopped
her by saying, " Not now, Hilda, it is a little
secret between us, and you must not tell
any one yet." The idea of having a secret
was quite enough to silence her, and before
the dinner was over, the whole thing had
passed from her mind.

The steamer did not arrive till nearly six
o'clock, she had been detained as supposed
by the fog; Arthur, however, was none the
worse, he was very glad to be home again,
and the first few days were passed in detail-

ing his school-boy exploits. Frank used to feel very proud of his brother, and longed to go back with him to school, to be able to join in all his gallant deeds. But before the holidays were over, there was a deep gloom thrown over our little circle, for George's state at length became too evident for his wife not to be aware of it.

It is strange that those nearest and dearest to us, are the last to see any danger; we might be almost within a few hours of death itself, and I believe those immediately about us would not perceive it, were it not for the ominous look of the doctor, or the unguarded remarks occasionally dropped by acquaintances. So it was with Rose, she seemed quite blind to her husband's state, and yet for months he had been gradually getting weaker and weaker, and each day saw some usual employment given up, from the want of strength to perform it, but she only thought him rather poorly, not very strong, getting fonder of sitting at home than he used to be. But death was dealing with him. That there could be a chance she should be parted from him, that she would be left to struggle on by herself, without George to look to for comfort and support, never for an instant crossed her mind. And so when the truth at length dawned, when one day old Dr. Davies came, and said he thought it his duty to tell her he considered her husband in a precarious state; it came like a death blow to her. It only needed the little wedge put in, the whole flood of misery and sorrow rushed into her heart, and it felt ready to burst. If she had been told he was dead, she could not have felt more agony than she did.

She sat down, and held her hands tight over her eyes, she could not have opened them, she could not think if her eyes were open; as it was, it was impossible for her to realise the idea of her beloved George's death, for that was what Dr. Davies' words implied, he knew he meant that, though he did not say so. How was she to believe it—how was she to face this dreadful blow? and yet there was no escape from it, she would have to bear it for her children's sake. At the thought of her children, she almost wished they might all die, that she might be quite alone, she thought she could bear it better if all went.

How long she sat there, she knew not; years seemed to have passed over her to judge from her face as she looked up on hearing some one come into the room, it was Arthur—he came to tell her, his father wanted her. She looked at the boy's bright beautiful face, and felt all a mother's strong love for her first born child come over her, she no longer wished him to die too; she got up instantly, and passed her hand through his jet black curly hair, and kissed him, and then went to her husband in his room, for he had not yet left it. For the last three weeks he had been unable to get up till the middle of the day, and this morning he felt he was not even able to do that, so he had sent for his wife, to ask her to do some trifle, that owing to his inability to do it, would otherwise be undone.

He looked at her as she came in, the sun was shining brightly, though it was a bitterly cold day, the snow on the roofs of the opposite houses made the light more dazzling. George asked her to draw down the blind, the glare was too great for him, but it enabled him to see the change in his wife's face. She drew the blind down, and took a chair and sat down by the side of his bed.

" What can I do for you, George ?" she could scarcely command her voice, for as she looked into his face, she felt the truth of Dr. Davies' words, and that he indeed would not be with her long ; how could she have been so blind ; if she had only known it sooner, how much more she would have been with him, but she would not leave him now for an instant, every moment it pleased God to spare him to her, she would devote to him. She laid her hand on his as . she spoke to him, it looked so thin, and so weak, as if he had not the power to lift it.

"Rose, dearest, something is wrong with you, what is it? You look as if some dire sorrow had fallen on you; you must tell me, I cannot bear to see you so."

"Do I, George?"

She tried to smile, but the attempt only made her do what she had been steeling herself against, and she burst into tears; she laid her head down, and wept long and bitterly, but after the paroxism had passed off, she felt better, as if she could talk, and she determined nothing again should make her give way, she would for his sake hide her grief.

"Dear George, you must think me very childish, but I feel nervous and uncomfortable this morning, and I am anxious about you, you don't get stronger. I think the winters here have been too cold for you, I should like, if possible, for us to get back to England; I think if you could get a curacy, however small, or anything there, would be better than staying here. I shall write to Wllliam, it is now ten years since I have heard of him, and I am sure he cannot be still unkindly disposed towards me; he will do something for you. I would never have thought of writing for myself, but for you I can, for I long to get you back to England," she talked very fast, and seemed to gain firmness as she went on. It was a new idea writing to her brother, and she thought after all, if they did go to England, George might get better; Dr. Davies did not tell her there was no hope, that was all her own idea, she had come to the conclusion that George was so very ill, but he might not be after all.

"No, Rose, don't buoy yourself up with a

vain hope, I now know the cause of your anxious looks, some one has told you that I am not long to be with you. Listen, my dearest wife, I have felt for some months I could not be with you much longer; I know myself the state I am in, and my sorrow at leaving you with those three poor children, and no one for you to look to, has, I fear, only increased the evil, and may cause you to be thrown alone into the wide world a little sooner than might have been. You must not give way so, for my sake you must bear up; and remember that God who sends the wound, will also send what is needful to heal it. It is hard for us to part, but you must try and be thankful that we have been spared to each other so long. Write to your brother, but not for me, write for yourself. Tell him I shall not be long with you to protect you, that you hope he has forgotten any annoyance your marriage may have· caused him; tell him all in fact that you can about yourself, and also from me, that if he is able, it would be a great comfort if he could come over, that I might feel I left you under his care and protection."

George stopped more from want of strength to go on, than from want of words; he felt a great relief, however, at his having spoken to his wife of his state, he could now think calmly of her future, and if her brother came to her, he could die peacefully, knowing her to be well cared for. He sent Rose away, for he heard Mr. Western coming up, and he thought it would spare her unnecessary sorrow to see any one just yet.

A few minutes after she left, Mr. Western came in, he had stopped to speak to his little favourite, Hilda. He was very little altered from when we first knew him, his hair may have been a little whiter, but nothing more. He came in, with his usual cheerful cheering face, and his " Well, Chichester, how are you?" but a sad expression soon chased the other away, for it was impossible for him not to see the change a few hours even had worked on his friend. No doubt, too, the excitement of his conversation with his wife had fatigued him, and given him a more languid look than usual.

A smile came over his countenance, and he opened his eyes slowly. " Much the same, I think, it does me good to see you though, and especially just now, I was wishing for you," he paused a moment, and then continued, " I have much to ask you to do for me, Western, for you must know, as well as my poor wife does now, that my days are numbered, and I think I have not many before I shall be called away from all those dear ones here. You know our history, and you know the deplorable state Rose will be left in if her brother does not help her. I have just sent her to write to him, she thought of doing so on my account, thinking English air might do me good, but I know, and I have endeavoured to make her know too, that I am beyond the aid of anything this world can do for me; but I wish her to write of herself, telling him her position, and I cannot help hoping that he will not disregard her request for his protection. I should wish, if I am spared a few days longer, for him to come over, that I might myself give her over to his care; but if anything sudden should occur to me, or should by any chance the letter be delayed—will you, Western," and George took hold of his hand, and raised himself up in his bed, " will you try and comfort my poor wife—will you try and protect her till she should hear from her brother—will you do for her what you would were she your daughter?"

Mr. Western could not reply for a few minutes, he was taken so by surprise, that he too felt as if till now he had never thought poor Chichester was anything more than rather delicate; he wondered he had not noticed the alteration in him; he had become as fond of him as if he had been a younger brother, he had grown so accustomed to him, that he could not picture to himself losing him. His voice shook as he pressed his hand, and replied, " I will, God bless you !" and he got up and left the room. He could not stay for fear of seeing the poor wife, and he could not have said anything to comfort her; he rushed out of the house for fear of meeting her, and went to see if old Dr. Davies could not give him some consolation and hope.

The Davies', from their first coming to Calais in the summer, had continued to do so every year till the last, when they determined to try the winter; they had become attached to the place and several of the people, and they felt happier in Calais than elsewhere. The daughter seemed almost as old as her father, she looked one of those people that never could have been young, or knew young feelings, but she was very good;

her face, though like old parchment, had a benign expression, there was always a word of sympathy ready for those in sorrow; she seemed to have gone through so much herself, that she knew what the sufferings of others must be.

But there Mr. Western gained no comfort by his visit. Dr. Davies more than confirmed his worst fears, he did not think George Chichester could last many days; he was then going to see him, and promised to call on Mr. Western on his way back. When he came, it was only to say he feared the days might prove but hours, for he was sinking rapidly, that the excitement he had gone through in the morning had exhausted him dreadfully.

The next day, however, he seemed better, he had slept calmly all night, and those who had never left him a moment, now went and laid down on a sofa; the children were in the next room, very quiet and very sad, their sorrow threw a temporary gloom over them, the boys were old enough to understand what their loss would be, but Hilda was more cross than unhappy, because they would not let her go and stay with her father.

It was nearly twelve o'clock, and a slight movement roused Rose instantly; she looked up, but saw George quite quiet, she thought perhaps he had turned, he looked asleep, she was at the further end of the room, and the blind was down. She continued to lay there about half an hour longer, but it was no rest to her, for she felt uneasy, so she got up and took her seat again by the side of the bed. George had never moved, she leant over him to kiss his forehead very gently for fear of disturbing him, her lips had scarcely touched him when she felt a shiver pass through her whole body, the knowledge that he was gone, came like an electric shock, when she was mercifully rendered unconscious and fell senseless over her husband's corpse.

We will not attempt to depict the widow's grief. The death of a friend causes a pang, how bitter then must be the sorrow of those who lose that which is dearest to them on earth! To feel you are parted for ever, that one you are daily accustomed to see, to consult in all difficulties, to fly to for comfort in all troubles, is taken from you, that you are no longer the first object of any one living, is a dreary, desolate feeling. There are some who have always felt that, but then they have never known what it is to be the first care and thought of another, and so the distress cannot be so great. It is more envy they suffer from, they envy the love and devotion payed to others, which they have never experienced.

Poor Rose! the blow fell with all its weight on her. She, for days, did not think of her position, she only thought of her loss! George was buried at the little churchyard in the Basse ville, just between Calais and the village of St. Pierre.

CHAPTER V.

DURING the years that Rose and George had passed since their marriage, William Fordyce had heard of them seldom. He had written to George's friend, Frank Bingham, to tell them of his father's death, and had written to him again about three years afterwards to let them know, through him, of his own marriage. Shortly aftewards, he had made an attempt to see his sister, and had gone down into Essex where George had held his curacy, and the only information he could glean, was that on the death of the late rector, Mr. Chichester had left, and they thought he had gone abroad. William then went to Frank Bingham, but he had also disappeared, and at his club it was believed he was in America.

Years had much diminished William's affection for Rose, and so having done all he imagined necessary, he quietly let the matter rest. Since his own marriage, Burwood had not been so completely his home. He had married the widow of a wealthy Scotch merchant, by whom she had one daughter about twenty, and on her becoming Lady Fordyce, she was anxious to get her daughter as well married as herself; and, therefore, William found he must give up his own pursuits till that was accomplished, and the season in London with a tour on the continent was the thing that must be gone through.

Three years saw Lady Fordyce's wishes gratified, and her daughter married, though not precisely as she wished. She met Captain Phillips at a ball given in the Kursaal at

Baden Baden, was engaged to him within a week, and they rushed off to London to get everything prepared for the marriage to take place immediately.

Captain Phillips was the youngest son of a Yorkshire squire, and, therefore, being under ban, he was on the look out for money; he succeeded in getting it, and with it—but we must not anticipate, for our story will necessarily throw us very much in the way of Mrs. Phillips, and therefore we will leave facts to speak for themselves.

Her daughter once out of her way, Lady Fordyce appeared less anxious about the London season, and willingly gave that up; but not so her continental tours—she was fond of new things and new places, and her husband was only too glad to gratify her in this as she was indifferent whether she travelled in the spring or autumn. They, therefore, went during the spring months abroad, and came back in time for Sir William to be ready on the 12th August at his little moor in Scotland, hoping he might be the first man to bring down the first grouse.

The winter George died, the Fordyces had determined to spend in the South; during their last autumn in Scotland, Lady Fordyce had caught a severe cold, and the medical men told her it was bronchitis she was suffering from, and that it would be advisable if she could winter at Nice, or any southern spot where she could be sheltered from easterly winds.

Doctors always recommend what their patients most like. They knew Lady Fordyce's travelling propensities, and they knew she would be so enchanted with the prospect, that their names would stand in her good books, and that they would be recommended to all her acquaintances. They took their fees, and she took their advice, and the beginning of November saw them as rapidly going southward, in their own comfortable chariot, as it was possible for good horses to carry them.

And so it happened that when Rose's letter reached Burwood, they were not there to receive it. No letters of any consequence being expected to be sent to them there during their absence, directions had been given that they were all to remain till, on the first of every month, Sir William's agent went down to see that all was going on properly, and for him to send such letters as he judged necessary to forward.

Rose's letter remained therefore for two or three weeks before being sent after her brother; and, in those days, posts did not go at the rate they do now, therefore another week elapsed before the letter actually came into Sir William's hands.

He had grown more like his father latterly, colder and more selfish. After reading the letter he turned to his wife, and said,

"I have received a letter from my sister.

What an unfortunate woman she seems! Her husband is dying at Calais, where he has been officiating for some years, and she has the prospect of being left with three children, and one hundred a-year. She will find it difficult to live on that."

This was all he said, as if he had been talking of his cook or housemaid, not of his own and only sister.

But Lady Fordyce, whose acquaintance we have but slightly made, was a warm-hearted person, on impulse. She did not do a good deed because it was right to do so, but only because she felt sorry at the moment for the person she meant to befriend; and, therefore, she had not thought a second before she exclaimed,

" Why, Sir William," she always called him Sir William, she thought it more imposing, and was proud of his being a baronet, " why, Sir William, we must go to her, poor thing, and see what can be done. We must go directly ;" and she got up, as if she was going to start then and there.

"Wait a minute, my dear, let me see ; why, the letter is dated more than a month since ; perhaps Chichester is dead by this. There is no use in going. Besides, you could not go now, you would just arrive in time to have the March winds cutting you to pieces."

Lady Fordyce was considerably older than her husband, and she occasionally showed that she thought herself wise in proportion. She was a tall, stately-looking person, and as she was standing up, waiting for Sir William to finish, he felt quite certain it would be useless to argue, and that if she meant to go, go she would. But he felt rather less cheerful after her saying, as she was leaving the room,

"I should have thought you had neglected your sister long enough when she had a husband, not to wish to continue doing so, when she doubly stands in need of comfort and support. I shall leave this evening; if you think it unnecessary, I can go without you."

They both started that night on their way to Calais, but, as to be of use, they had to go quicker than was quite consistent with ease, Lady Fordyce's warm sympathy was gradually cooling down, and it was Sir William's turn then to urge her on. It was, however, in not an over-charitable mood that saw her get out of their carriage at Dessin's Hotel, where they put up.

As soon as they were in their rooms, a porter was sent to the Consul, to enquire if he was at home, and if so, if he would take the trouble to call on Sir William Fordyce, or, if more convenient, if he should go to him.

The answer came in Mr. Western himself. He knew immediately who had sent for him, and guessed their motive. He rather dreaded the interview, for he knew he would have to detail much that was sad and painful for him to discuss; but he was determined to lose no opportunity of furthering Rose's interests.

On his being announced, Sir William, who was alone, got up and said, "I must introduce myself to you, Mr. Western, as the brother of Mrs. Chichester, which, I hope, will prove sufficient apology for my troubling you to call; but Lady Fordyce and myself have but within this hour arrived, as a letter from my sister, telling me of her anxiety about her husband, and requesting me to come to her, only reached me last week in Italy, where we were passing the winter. Owing to the delay, I feared to send to the address she gave me, till I ascertained how matters stood with her—whether poor Chichester was still living or not, and how she herself was; and it is to ask you to give me all the information you can, that I took the liberty of sending for you."

"I am sorry, Sir William, to be the medium through which you become acquainted with the heavy blow your sister has sustained. Poor George Chichester has been dead a month; he died within two days of the letter you so recently received being written. She is still here, and is, indeed, in much want of your aid and protection. Not knowing where you were, I wrote also to Burwood, telling you of his death, and his earnest wish that you would forget the past, and only think of her as your sister, and not his wife. But I suppose that letter has never reached you. I promised to do what I would have done had she been my own daughter, till I was able to place her under your care; and it is a great responsibility removed from me now; and I am sure, knowing you are here on her account, will greatly tend to alleviate her sorrow. Will you like me to go and prepare her for seeing you?"

"Thank you; I really should be extremely obliged. And, perhaps, you would come back and tell me whether she would like to see me at once, or wait till to-morrow, as it is some years since we have met, and she may feel a little agitated."

This was all said in a formal, pompous, matter-of-fact way, that by no means won Mr. Western's good opinion ; but there was no use in his trying to battle against a man's own nature, and he felt certain William Fordyce had no heart, so there was not the slightest object in his staying there to try and touch what did not really exist.

As soon as a few more unmeaning remarks had been passed, Mr. Western got up to leave. Just as he was going out of the room, Lady Fordyce opened the door and came in. Sir William introduced him, but he hurried out, for the lady's face was not prepossessing, and he dreaded hearing something that might tend to lessen poor Rose's chance of future peace. So before she could say a word to stop him, he was gone. Gone, to try and prepare the poor, forlorn widow to receive a cold, pompous brother, and an unpleasant-looking sister-in-law.

" I wish, Sir William, you had sent to tell me Mr. Western was here, I should very much have liked to have seen him, and heard all he said. The maid who came into my room just now, told me the English clergyman had died about a month ago, so I fear your poor sister must be in a very desolate state. She told me all the English here were very grieved, and that they could not do enough to show his widow their respect for her husband. What have you settled with him?—when shall you go to see her? I think, perhaps, you had better go without me, as a perfect stranger is never very welcome in sorrow," a touch of her good feeling was coming back.

Sir William told her that was all arranged, and there was nothing to do but wait patiently till they again saw Mr. Western.

We will follow him in his visit to Mrs. Chichester. It was not far from the Hotel where the Fordyces were, to her lodgings, so he had not time to arrange his thoughts, and what he should say; and it was just as well, for it would have cost him some trouble to decide, and then there would have been no probability of his putting his words in the form he intended.

How often people write out what they have to say, learn it by heart, and when the moment comes, the memory has not retained a syllable, and there they are, groping about in the dark as it were, till chance puts an idea in their way, they grapple hold of it, and make a speech worth a dozen of the set formal one.

So he walked in, and found the mother and children altogether.

A widow's dress generally calls forth some pity for the wearer, whatever she may be, for it is a melancholy-looking garb, though very often the sympathy may be thrown away. But Rose looked particularly interesting in hers. The widow's cap, on her, did not look like an advertisement of her being free to accept an eligible offer, as it does, and is, with many. She might have sat for a picture of grief; her youth was all gone, and there were lines under the eyes that told of the mental agony she had gone through.

She was sitting near the fire, leaning her face against her hand; the other hand was resting on Hilda's neck, who was sitting on a stool by her, playing with a new toy Dr. Davies had sent her; a little mouse, that, when wound up, would run about by itself; and her amusement was making Don try and believe it was real, and that he must catch it. Don was sitting watching her, and looking as if he could not believe it, even to please her. Arthur was sitting at the table reading, and Frank was by the window watching and listening to a discussion that was taking place between an old woman and a soldier; from the occasional laugh it was evident they were not quarrelling, but to judge from their gesticulations, you would have thought they must be in an intense rage, that every word was instead of a blow.

As Mr. Western looked at the little group, his heart sank within him. What a brother it was she had to depend on, and that he had now to tell her had arrived, and hoped she was quite well! However, it might turn out better, he would not give up all hope till he saw what Sir William meant to do for her. He did not think there was any occasion to delay telling her immediately of his arrival; just at present, nothing would excite her for joy or sorrow, and so he said, almost immediately after going in,

"I have had news of your brother, Mrs. Chichester; in short, he is in Calais, and sent for me as soon as he arrived.

He is at Dessin's, where I have just left him."

"Is he coming here, then?" said Rose. "I suppose I ought to feel very glad he has come, but I don't. It seems like the first step to my leaving Calais, and that thought makes me very miserable."

"He won't come here till I go back and tell him when you would wish to see him. His wife is with him."

"His wife!" exclaimed Rose. "Is he married then? Oh, if he is married, I cannot expect him to think of me. When was he married?"

"I don't know anything about that," said Mr. Western, smiling at the notion of William having told him about his marriage, "but she is, I should say, some years older than him; she looks about fifty, whereas, I suppose, he is not more than two or three-and-forty."

"No; I suppose that is his age. Does he

seem happy? But I must not keep you here, asking questions, if he is waiting for you. But tell me, Mr. Western, is his wife coming with him ?"

"I don't know; would you rather she did not? Because, perhaps, I might manage it."

"I think I should prefer his coming alone. Did you see her? what sort of person is she ?"

Mr. Western, not caring to give his hastily formed opinion of her, said he had but seen her for an instant as he was going out of the room, and should not know her again were he to meet her.

"Who are you going to bring to see mamma ?" said Hilda.

"A new uncle for little Hilda," answered Mr. Western.

"Well, then, I don't want a new uncle, or a new anything, I like old things best; and I like you better than a new uncle. So tell him to go, and not come to see mamma."

This speech did not sound very promising for the reception William was to get from his little niece ; but he merely patted her head, and told her she must be kind to her uncle, because her mamma loved him.

This seemed some sort of excuse for an intruder, so Hilda turned her attention back to Don and the mouse, doubly intent on making a fool of the dog.

When he had gone, Mrs. Chichester turned to Arthur, and said, " You have heard so little of any of your relations, my dear boy, that, perhaps, you, till lately, hardly knew I had a brother. I ought, perhaps, to have told you more about him, but circumstances so completely separated us, that we have been like strangers for years. Your father's last wish was, that I should place myself and you three children under his care, and as he wished it, it was sufficient for me. I wrote some time since, and he now only has come to us.

"You are old enough, Arthur, to understand that much of your future will depend on him; and you will try therefore, I am sure, for my sake, to make your uncle form a favorable opinion of you. You are a little haughty in your manner, dear child, especially with strangers; but I am sure you will not give way to any feeling of pride in the present case. What I am saying, Frank, I must repeat almost to you, excepting the last few words; but you are younger, and, I know, much given to imitate your brother. I want you now, however, to be yourself, and act towards your uncle as your own feelings dictate."

"Certainly, mamma," said Frank, "I will try and behave properly to my uncle."

"Well," said Arthur, "of course I will behave properly, too; but I think he might have taken the trouble to have come to you a little sooner, and I don't see that there is much to thank him for yet. But don't be afraid, mamma ; at all events, for your sake, I won't tell him so."

Arthur certainly did not, by his reply, tend to remove his mother's anxiety about the way he might choose to behave. She had known him, nearly two years ago, whilst paying a visit with Mr. Western at some English family's house in Calais, because he was not offered a chair, and treated like a guest, take up his cap and walk out. She felt certain Frank would bear and forbear, for his was naturally a gentle, forgiving disposition; but she dreaded Arthur marring his own prospects by some burst of pride, should his uncle call it forth by any casual patronizing speech.

How little pleasure we feel at the prospect of meeting those, no matter how dear they may be, or have been, to us, if we are about to solicit a favour; or, without having to do that, feel we shall be dependant on them, for whatever generosity they may be disposed to show.

Nothing is so galling, nothing so hard to bear as dependance, and how rarely one is so, without being momentarily reminded of it. It may be one is more tenacious, and every light word spoken without intending to hurt, or perhaps even spoken without any thought, if it should touch on the one point, how deeply it will cut. Why is it in our own country poverty is looked on as a disgrace? People are ashamed to be poor, they will do any thing, sacrifice any comfort, pinch themselves in actual necessaries, rather than the world should not believe them much richer than they are; but it does not even apply to those of small means, but the very richest, if they have twenty thousand a year they wish it to be thought that they have thirty; they are but too frequently gratified, for people love so to exaggerate, and it is pleasant to be thought on intimate terms with very wealthy people, so that their friends are ever ready to gratify them, and yet themselves always exclaiming that they cannot afford this or that. You may be an honest, upright, truthful man, but what good can that do you? if you are poor you cannot entertain your friends, you cannot make any great display in your establishment, and so you are not worth knowing. But suddenly, have some kind-hearted godfather die and leave you great wealth, you will then find you may be all that is despicable and vicious, but you will have the world to support you, and proud, too, of your acquaintance.

Rose had been trying to school herself to the meeting with her brother as she had endeavoured to school her children, but she could as yet not bring herself to any quiet thoughts. At one moment, she was thinking what she should say to him, and then as she pictured him before her she could only see him as a young man coming home from college and herself a child. The next moment she was walking with her husband, walking in the garden belonging to the little vicarage they went to after their marriage, there was no use in trying to think of the present—she could not, her brother had so completely belonged to the past, that she could not identify him with the present.

An hour must have elapsed since Mr. Western left—an hour is not long if passed pleasantly; but when we are watching for any one, or anxious about any thing, how slowly the minutes pass, each one seems ten; if you look at the clock it always seems where it was the last time you looked, which appeared to you at least a quarter of an hour ago.

Rose thought it was so late now they would not come that night. She sent Hilda to bed, not quite sorry to have her safely out of the way in case they should come. She had but just returned into the sitting-room when she heard footsteps on the stairs; there was no street door with a knocker to give the inmates notice of the approach of visitors; they walked in at a large gate, turning then into the house on the left, came straight up the stairs; and, therefore, a moment more and her brother and Mr. Western entered. He thought it would be rather a comfort to Rose that he should go in with him; he was always thoughtful and kind to others, so he merely said, "Mrs. Chichester, I came up just to show Sir William Fordyce the way, and to run off again, for I have much business to get through to-night," and he was gone. But it answered his purpose and, formed a sort of break to the meeting.

William went up to his sister and said, "It is so long, Rose, since we met, I suppose you would scarcely know me; you, too, are changed. Dear me! how very much altered you are; and are these your boys? Come and say how d'ye do to me," this was addressed to

Arthur and Frank, who went up and shook hands with him.

Rose felt less agitated now her brother was there than she had been whilst expecting him, she begged him to sit down by her, and before talking of herself to tell her a little of his own affairs, of his marriage, and who his wife was. William, in his cold way, told her what we already know, he did not at all seem to understand why she could possibly be interested in any thing relating to him.

After his having been talking of things that had no reference to Rose, or the cause of his visit, he said, "Now I think we had better discuss the future a little. I wish to know what your plans are, and in what way I may be able to help you to carry them out. Supposing you send the children to bed, we shall be able to speak more freely."

Arthur jumped up and banged out of the room at the disrespect he imagined shown him, Frank went up and wished his mother and uncle good night and left them.

"That eldest boy does not seem to have the mildest of tempers, I am afraid you have spoilt him," her brother remarked rather drily.

Rose was vexed beyond measure, she had so dreaded something of the sort, and she scarcely knew what excuse she could make for him. "Arthur has been so accustomed to be treated as much older than he really is, that I fancy he felt hurt at being considered too much of a child to remain, but I am very sorry he should have given way so to his temper," she said.

"Well, never mind him now; tell me what you thought of doing. I am really very sorry for the loss you have had, but you know poor Chichester was never very strong. Had he been ill long when you wrote."

" I only knew of his danger a day or two before," replied Rose, trying to stifle her sobs, for the mere mention of her husband had quite upset her.

"Your letter never reached me till last week or I should have been here sooner. Lady Fordyce had been ordered to winter abroad, and owing to your letter not being forwarded immediately, I did not receive it till it was a month old." He paused for a minute or two, and then made a third attempt about the future. "Do you wish to remain here, or go to England; or are you in communication with any of your husband's family, whose advice you might wish to follow?"

He spoke in such a calm, unconcerned sort of manner that it threw a great damp over Rose, she felt she could not look on him as one that would be interested in her and hers, that he merely was acting as he thought it his duty to do by so near a relative, but that his heart had nothing to do with the matter. She told him she thought for her boys' sake it would be better for her to go to England, and that she knew and had heard nothing of or from George's relations, otherwise she would have preferred remaining in Calais where she had been so happy.

"Of course," said Sir William, "I shall be happy to help you to the best of my means, and I think, too, it will be wiser for you to return to your country and place the boys at school. I am not sure when Lady Fordyce will be ready to leave, but I dare say you can arrange to go over with us. I will go back to the hotel and hear all she says. She begged me to give her regards to you, and say she should have come with me, but she thought you would prefer seeing me alone, but she will call at any time you feel disposed to receive her."

"Oh tell her," said Rose, to whom this message appeared doubly kind from the comparison with her brother's manner, "that I shall be so glad to know her, and that as it is too late for her to come out to-night, and that I daresay she is very tired, I hope she will come in the morning."

Rose felt relieved when her brother was gone, glad the meeting was over, and glad that the restraint his manner to her, caused her to feel, whilst he was present, was removed. How different he was to the good-hearted, joyous being she remembered him. But of course years do make a great difference in us all, more almost in feeling than appearance, for generally you can trace the features, and often the same expression in a face we knew young, and now see old, but rarely we recognize the same disposition or taste. What we liked in our childhood, we contemn in our youth, what we loved in our youth, we grow dissatisfied with in our old age.

But it is well it is so, for we should but be more exposed to sorrow, and it has pleased Providence to give each human being as heavy a load as any desire to bear; for the trials of others, that appear but trifles to us in comparison with our own, are in truth as severe to them as our's are to us, we simply don't think so, because we never take into consideration all the adjuncts of another's troubles.

There may be two persons, equally condemned to some dreadful illness, the one shall be very rich, the other very poor; you will say how can that be called an equal trial to each—why the rich one can have all the comforts that wealth can give, the poor one must suffer and want as well perhaps for actual necessaries. Very true, but the rich one will repine that all their wealth is useless, the only thing they want is health, and their money may actually become an extra source of vexation to them; the poor one will feel more resigned, from having none of the tamperings that wealth gives, and feel also that had they all the wealth of

Crœsus, it could not benefit them. I do most firmly believe, that there is a just distribution of happiness and sorrow to all mankind.

CHAPTER VI.

" DID you ever know any one contented, my dear, for I never did, enough is always a little more than what they have, besides people, I tell you, never are contented." This was addressed by Sir William Fordyce to his wife, at breakfast, the morning after his visit to his sister.

They had been discussing her affairs, and what was to be done. Sir William thought if she went over to England, and took a small cottage near some town, where she could put the boys at school, and that if he added to her income of a hundred a year, another hundred, she might be very comfortable. It was on Lady Fordyce suggesting £200 a year was not enough to be contented on, that her husband made the above remark.

"Perhaps you may be right with regard to some people, Sir William," she replied, "and as I have not yet seen your sister, I cannot judge; but I should have thought she would do her best to be happy in whatever state of life she might be placed in. Of course, I only speak from what I should think of a person who being brought up as she was, was never heard to murmur by one belonging to her of the great changes she had when she married."

"Well, for the matter of that, she had no opportunity, for her letters were always burnt unopened by my father, therefore we don't know what she said, though I am not wishing to make you think she was dissatisfied, only we never knew whether she was, or was not."

"Well, at all events I will get ready and

go with you at once, and then I can judge of her myself," said Lady Fordyce, and she got up and left the room, returning in a short time ready to walk with her husband, and make the acquaintance of her new sister-in-law. She fortunately had one of her amiable impulsive humours on her, and the distance from the Hotel to the Rue Française, was too short for it to have time to wear away, added to which the tone her husband continued to talk of his sister in, tended rather to increase her good feelings towards her than otherwise.

On getting to her lodgings, having in vain hunted for a bell, or a servant of some description to announce them, they walked up, and after hearing a gentle " Come in," to their knock at the door, they opened it. Mrs. Chichester rose up the moment she saw her brother and his wife, and went forward to receive the latter with a degree of warmth she could not account for, for there was nothing attractive in Lady Fordyce's appearance; she was middle aged, rather above the ordinary height, stout and heavy looking. She was fair, with small eyes, a bad nose, and a very ugly mouth, her teeth rather projecting; but she went towards Rose and put her arms round her, and kissing her on the forehead, merely said " Poor thing," but those two words spoke more to the heart than the most elaborate speech, and Rose felt gratified to her for her kind manner. Lady Fordyce's eyes were full of tears, and she turned to the children to pass the awkward minutes that generally follow after a meeting of that kind.

The little scene had not been lost on the children, Arthur came forward immediately, and held out his hand, and looked up in her face, he was going to say something, but before he could do so, she exclaimed, " What a beautiful boy, what would I not give to have had a child like this?" A slight cloud passed over his face, which she noticed, and interpreted aright; it soon cleared off, and she said, "but beauty is little unless you are good, and you look good, I am sure you are a comfort to your poor mamma."

"I hope I shall be some day soon," Arthur said.

Frank was standing by, and he took hold of Lady Fordyce's hand, and said, "I mean to be a comfort to my mamma, and make her happy again."

She turned towards him, and putting her hand on his head, said, "Indeed, my dear child, you look as if you would make every one happy that you were with. You may well be proud of your boys," she added, turning to Mrs. Chichester, who was talking to her brother.

"I must introduce you to my little girl," said Rose, taking Hilda by the hand, and leading her up to her sister-in-law.

"Why, I did not know you had another,

Sir William only mentioned your two boys to me."

"Well, I did not know it myself," said Sir William, "this little lady did not appear last night, and Rose never mentioned her."

Lady Fordyce sat down, and was going to lift Hilda on to her lap, but she would not be lifted up, and looking up in her aunt's face, said, "I don't know you yet."

"Well no, but perhaps you will soon know me, and then you will come and sit on my lap, wont you? I won't ask you to come till you wish it."

Hilda made no answer, but moved off to a corner of the room where Don was lying; she sat down by the side of him, and probably confided to him all her opinions of her new relations. We must leave them to each other, and turn our ears to the more serious conversation of their elders.

Arthur, remembering his uncle's remark last night, determined not to lay himself open to a repetition of it, and therefore he went up to his mother, and said, "I will go round to Mr. Western's, mamma, and Frank will go with me, unless you have any objection ; have you any message ?"

" No, Arthur, only my love to him ; take care of Frank, do not be late for dinner."

Arthur and Frank said good morning, and went out. There was a pause for a few minutes, at last Lady Fordyce said, " You must be anxious to get your two boys at a good school, are you not ? You would not like them to be brought up entirely here."

" Oh, no," said Rose, " this place is well enough for children, but not when they begin to get to boyhood. Arthur has been for eighteen months at a clergyman's near London, but of course I was not able to send him this quarter. It is my wish to be able to live in England for their sakes ; but I fear England will be far beyond my income."

" I was talking to Lady Fordyce this

morning," said her brother, " and about what we thought it would be best for you to do. I will double your income, which will make it two hundred a year, and I think if you live carefully, you ought to make that do.   I should advise your taking a small house in the neighbourhood of London, and then when settled in it, you can decide what you best like with regard to your boys."

"I am very much obliged, William, for your generous offer; and I will do all in my power to enable me to give my boys a thorough education.   Arthur is very clever, and I think, will, when older, be able to make his own way in the world; but Frank is so delicate, that I dread the hardships of a school for him, I have hitherto kept him at home on that account."

Lady Fordyce, during the last few minutes, had been intently watching Hilda, she was a strange child, and had evidently taken her fancy.   She was apparently holding an animated conversation with Don, and what seemed to suit her most was, having it entirely to herself—Don only vouchsafing a friendly grunt every now and then, or licking her face, when she put it down near enough to him, without his having the trouble to lift his head.   Don was older than when we first made his acquaintance, and therefore less active, and more given to look out for comfort and quiet.

Lady Fordyce had been ruminating on the child's probable future; an idea crossed her, and it had no sooner done so, than the idea became a wish, and from a wish to a desire; but she was interrupted in her castles in the air, by her husband saying: " My dear, if my sister settles to return toEngland, don't you think it would be advisable she should do so as soon as possible ?"

Lady Fordyce directed her answer to Mrs. Chichester, she did not quite like the dunning part Sir William apparently meant her to

play in her own affairs, so she said, " If you
feel equal to the journey, I think you would
like having your brother to take all the
trouble of travelling off your hands, and of
course we could delay going till your pre-
parations were made—you have no objection, I
am sure, Sir William ?"

" Oh, none at all, my dear," answered Sir
William, anything but pleased at the prospect
of either the prolonged stay in Calais, or the
travelling with three children in his train ;
but he never attempted a direct contradiction
to his wife, when she had arranged any
plan, so he only ventured to add, " 1 suppose,
Rose, you will not require more than a couple
of days to prepare."

Rose, to whom the departure was altogether
new, seemed to hesitate ; to her, two days
seemed quite insufficient to get herself and
her children ready to leave in, especially as it
was a final departure ; but she thought it
would not do to give up the benefit of her

brother's protection, especially as she remembered how anxious George had been
about it, and she did not like to throw cold
water on Lady Fordyce's kind proposition ;
but her sister-in-law came to her aid, and
said, "It is quite out of the question for you
to be ready in two days. This is Saturday,
supposing we settle to leave next Thursday ;
do you think that will be too soon ?"

" I can be quite ready by Thursday, but it,
is taxing your kindness too far to wish you
to remain so long, however great the benefit
of your escort might be. I am sure we shall
get the journey over safely ; I have friends
here who would see me on board, and so you
must not think of remaining."

" Indeed, my dear Mrs. Chichester, I shall
not allow you to go alone with three young
children. If Sir William cannot remain, I
will ; and he can go over if necessary, and
come back for us, so say no more about it."

Sir William, who had no notion of being

unnecessarily sea sick, and as the weather was none of the mildest, *he* did say no more about it, but quickly made up his mind to remain till Thursday; but Rose could not but express her thanks to Lady Fordyce, and assure her how she should ever remember all her sympathy and kindness.

They rose to go, and Hilda jumped up and went to her aunt, and said, " Good-bye; next time you come, perhaps I will sit on your lap." This piece of condescention on her part was received as it was meant, and Lady Fordyce felt very pleased, and the wish that had taken hold of her, only gained firmer root.

The next day, Sunday, Mr. Western came, as had been his custom since poor Chichester's death, and fetched the widow and her three children to go to church. It had been a hard trial for Rose the first time she went, to see another standing in the place where she had never seen any but her own husband;

but each successive Sunday it had been less difficult to bear. Time will alleviate every sorrow; it is well it does, or we should sink under them. But to-day Rose felt very sad, she knew it would be her last; she would perhaps never again return to Calais, where she had passed so many happy years, and latterly so many sorrowful months. It is strange, but yet true, that sorrow will endear a place to us almost as much as pleasure; there is a sad clinging feeling which we cannot account for, but which yet exists.

After church was over, she went her usual walk on the ramparts, and then told Mr. Western of her future plans—all her brother and sister-in-law had said, the latter's kindness in not allowing her to go back to England alone, and, therefore, the reason that she must leave so soon, so as not to delay them longer than actually necessary—her brother's ideas of what she ought to do, how and where she ought to live, his increase to her income, in fact all she could call to mind as having passed on the previous day, she related.

Mr. Western said little, but thought the more; however, he determined never again to judge another by their faces, for he evidently had sadly misjudged Lady Fordyce; she appeared, from Rose's account, far more feeling and thoughtful than her brother had been. He thought a hundred a year a mean, shabby annuity, for an only brother with upwards of eight thousand a year to an only sister with nothing; but he yet hoped from Lady Fordyce's conduct that she would befriend Rose, and so not leave her upon such an income.

"I don't know what I shall do when you are gone," said Mr. Western, "I shall feel quite lost."

"I hope we may soon meet again," continued Rose, "you will, I hope, be before long obliged to go over to England, and it will be one of the very few pleasures I shall look forward to, will be meeting you again. You have been such a kind friend to me, that I almost feel as if in leaving you here, I was parting from all that felt interested in me and mine."

"You must not think that, for you will find many friends in England, and plenty will be ready to take interest in you. I wrote some time ago to Frank Bingham but I have not had any answer, I fancy he cannot have returned from America; I shall write again after you have left."

They talked on for some little time longer, when Mr. Western walked back with his little party, and left them at their own door. He felt unusually out of sorts now the parting was so near, he felt how sadly he should miss them when they were gone. He was old, too, now, and did not care about new friends, he liked the faces he was accustomed to; and as he walked back to his own house the idea of his resigning occurred to him. What should he do all alone, after being accustomed daily to have the children with him? after being accustomed to go in and out of the Chichesters' house like his own. No, he would resign, but he would say nothing about it till they were all safely settled in England; but the determination soothed him, and he soon regained his usual cheerfulness.

The few days previous to the departure passed rapidly; they were so busy making purchases and packing, that night came much too soon for their accommodation.

The boys were in high spirits at the prospect of change, most people are, but to a child there is a great charm in novelty.

Hilda had made friends with Lady Fordyce, but not so with her uncle. She did not feel by any means attracted towards him, and she did not attempt to appear to be so.

Don did not seem at all to understand what was going on, he had never been witness to such an extensive preparation for a journey ; the outside of his observations had been a portmanteau and carpet-bag, he could not conceive anything beyond it.

On Wednesday, the day before they were to leave, Sir William and Lady Fordyce came in, and Hilda was in a very animated conversation with her mother and Mr. Western. Whatever the subject might have been, the little girl evidently was getting quite beyond the reach of persuasion.

A child always knows instinctively where it can safely look for support, so the sight of Lady Fordyce was like a ship to a drowning man. Her eyes were looking larger than ever as she made a bound towards her on coming in.

" Aunt," she cried out, " mamma and Mr. Western say I can't take Don with me. Can't I, aunt ? Because, if I can't, I don't want to go to England. I will stop with Don here. *Do* say I may take him."

" My dear, Don is a very large dog, and I think your mamma will find him very troublesome. Don't you think, too, Don will be happier himself to stay with Mr. Western ?"

" Certainly," said Sir William, " the child is mad to want to take that big brute with her !"

" I don't care what you say," Hilda said, turning to her uncle; " he is not a big brute; are you, my darling, Don ?" and the child went to the dog, and laid her head on his, and broke forth in a torrent of tears.

Lady Fordyce went up to her; she felt the first appeal had been made to her, that the child had looked to her to get her object attained, and she thought it would strengthen the apparent liking that Hilda already felt for her, if she were the means of her wish being gratified; besides, it pained her to see the little thing sobbing so.

So she put one hand on the dog's head and the other on Hilda's, and said : " Listen to me, Hilda, and you, too, Don, for I must speak to you both," this was enough to make Hilda all attention, that Don was to be considered in some way, at all events. " Would you love me very much, Hilda, if I were to take Don to England, and keep him for you at my house in the country, and for you to come and see him whenever you liked ?   And would you, Don, behave very properly if I took you ?"

It is better to take the inch if you cannot get the ell, and so Hilda considered the offer, and though only half pleased, said,

" Yes, I will love you, and you shall take Don ; and I know he will be good, he is always good.   Mamma, aunty says I shall have Don.   Do you hear, Mr. Western, I may take Don, I told you I would not leave him !"

Mr. Western, who had risen to go, was

not quite sure whether to believe it or not, and so, turning to Lady Fordyce, said, "I think you will repent of your offer to take such a charge; but Hilda, perhaps, may forget it by to-morrow."

Sir William was quite indifferent as to a dog more or less in his kennel, and only thought of the additional live stock to the party the next day.

Rose had been with Hilda in the morning to take leave of old Dr. Davies and his daughter, and the boys had gone there now, and were just coming in as their aunt and uncle were going out. So, with a " Mind you are ready in good time to-morrow," they each went their way.

Mr. Western was to return during the afternoon to take Rose to the cemetery; the children were to go also, and so as soon as they were altogether and alone, Rose went to get herself and Hilda ready. She was going to enjoy, for the last time, the pleasure of being near all that had been so dear to her on earth.

We will not follow them in their farewell visit to the grave of the husband and father. There are very few, if any of us, who have not had some loved object snatched away from us by death, and therefore we know what an aching void there is in our hearts, when we look on the earth, and know that what we so idolized in life is now buried there; but with the pain there is a deep gratitude that we are permitted to see their last resting-place, that we were permitted to tend, and watch, and soothe them in their last moments, that their eyes closed looking at us, praying God to bless us, that ours was the last hand theirs held.

None can know and appreciate the real blessings of attending the death-bed of a beloved friend or relative, but those who have been denied it. For a paid servant to be where you ought to have been, for you to be ignorant of their last wishes and last words, —oh, none know what that sorrow is but those who have felt it !

The last hours spent in Calais were very heavy ones to all, and as the parting was to be, each were anxious it should be over. The morning of Thursday saw all our party on board the steamer, Don and all, Mr. Western was there too that he might see the last of them; the warning bell had just rang, one last grasp of Rose's hand and a hurried " God bless you," and he jumped on. shore. She and the children watched him, but he did not turn round to look at them, but hurried back to his little home ; they felt leaving him very much, but there was a certain excitement in the going to their own country again, that took away the sting of parting.

We should never pity those who go as we do those who remain, the former find it impossible to brood over their pain, new things, new places, new people, all take part in their thoughts; whereas, the latter go back to the same things, the same places, the same people, but miss the absent one in all. Everything reminds them of their absence, the very streets look deserted, the desolate feeling within one spreads to all and every thing around. So felt Mr. Western as he crossed the market place, which was begining to move with life; but to him it was empty, he never saw the town look so dull and dreary, and yet the bright morning sun was shining and making the whole place look more cheerful than usual.

CHAPTER VII.

On their first arrival, through Lady Fordyce's arrangements, all went down to Burwood. It seemed to Rose like a dream, it seemed impossible that since she was last there, she had become a wife, a mother, and a widow!

The place was very much altered. Shortly before Sir John Fordyce's death he had enlarged and improved it considerably, and alterations were still going on in the grounds. The house was built of white stone, in the Italian style; in the front was a large portico that a carriage drove under and you entered at

once into a very fine lofty hall, which, however, was as much spoilt as it could be, by
bad, glaring-looking pictures covering the
walls—one which looking more unpleasant
than any of the others, was a picture supposed to be a portrait of Cardinal Wolsey,
his scarlet robe making one's eyes ache painfully, but poor Sir William imagined he
knew a good picture, and of course thought
all was perfect; his friends never liked to un-
deceive him.

The floor was covered with a magnificent
Turkey carpet, and in the centre stood a very
handsome billiard-table. On entering the
hall, the opposite side of it presented three or
four doors to view, as also on the left; these
doors led to the different sitting-rooms,
which all communicated with each other.

We will enter from the first door on our
left hand, and that leads us at once into what
was called the blue drawing-room. There were
two drawing-rooms, one blue, the other·

yellow, so called from the coloured drapery and furniture. In the first room, which is the largest, there is a glass door leading into a very pretty conservatory, full of bright looking flowers, and a strong smell of heliotrope; the two rooms might be one, they are so open into each other; there are doors between, but they are glass, and they open and fold back so far, that unless you looked for them, you would think they belonged to the wall.

All the windows were bowed, and the walls and ceilings were beautifully painted a mixture of arabesque and flowers; but there was nothing homely in these rooms, they evidently were not for every day use; there was a stiff, formal look about them, that you felt on going into them, as if you merely went to look at them, and not inhabit them; like a very handsome new dress, you were uncomfortable in it, and felt it was for other people's admiration, not your own.

There was a door in the yellow room, which was the farthest off, that on opening, did not much extend one's information, for you only came against another door. Why double doors were made, I know not, but there they were; on opening the second, you entered a library, and a perfect one of its kind. I must describe it fully, for with it we may have more to do. It was a square room with doors and windows occupying three sides of it, and the fire place the fourth, but between the doors were book cases filled with books, of a heavy, dry, old fashioned description; there were two writing tables, one in the middle of the room, the other standing on one side of the fire place, both well covered with necessaries.

A very large, comfortable sofa of morocco leather, with a deep back and two sides, the same height, and all being straight up, two arm-chairs to match, with a few others more or less comfortable. Where there was a spare piece of paper, hung some execrable picture, horrible copies of Byron, Walter Scott, the Empress Catherine, and Mary, Queen of Scots, sadly disfiguring the room. Two windows, both down to the ground, and opening into the garden, gave it a cheerful look.

We now go through the door facing the one we entered the room by, and come again against another, which having opened, we find ourselves in a large, lofty dining-room, the three windows at the end of the room being built in a large bow, thereby adding much to the size of the room. It was furnished with heavy, massive carved oak; over the mantle piece is a life-like portrait of Sir William as he now is, the only really decent picture in the house.

Leading out of the dining, is the breakfast-room, a light, pretty room, with white paper, and cherry coloured furniture, with a few pictures, hung so that the light comes on them in charity to hide them. All these rooms have doors opening into the hall, and the windows into the garden. A wide staircase led you out of the hall up into a long gallery, along which were situated the bedrooms.

Old Sir John Fordyce had the peculiar fancy of having the bed-rooms numbered in the way one sees at an hotel, his own commencing with number one; and the numbers still remained, and the rooms were often designated by them. When no company was staying in the house, the library was used as the sitting room. It is in the former we must go to see who is in it.

Rose, and her children, and Don had been at Burwood about a fortnight, and though she enjoyed much the quiet and freedom from care that the constant thought of £ s d always entails, she felt she could not remain for ever; she must not let her boys be losing more time, and so she had determined this morning to tell Lady Fordyce that she thought it time for her to settle in her own home.

Rose was standing looking out at one of the library windows watching her boys; they were trying how they could walk in and about the little beds of flowers, without touching them.

The flower garden in front of the window was one of those stiff, ugly things, called an Italian garden, little turrils and twists of beds all bordered with box, cut in the most prim, stiff fashion, and amongst them little narrow miniature walks covered with different coloured sand. The whole having a walk of about a foot in width, wide in comparison with the others, surrounding it, and outside that again a white stone border forming scollops round these strange looking things. The whole was like a view presented to you on looking through a kaleidescope. Hilda was not visible, she was last seen with Don, and trying to make him walk on his hind legs by the side of her.

Rose was waiting for Lady Fordyce to come in, as she usually did about eleven o'clock, having concluded all her household arrangements for the day. Rose had a great dislike to talking business, so the time seemed very long with the anticipation before her till her sister-in-law appeared. When she did come in, she began talking of different matters that had no interest for Mrs. Chichester, and Lady Fordyce seeing she looked as if something was making her thoughtful, exclaimed, " Is any thing the matter, Rose? you look like a person who had just heard some disagreeable news."

" No," said Rose, " but I have been think-ing this last day or two, that I must not delay making my arrangements for the future, and I wished to speak to you about it; we have been here a fortnight, and really we must settle at once where and how we had better live ; for I feel that the boys are losin their time, and I, too, cannot feel comfortable till I am fixed in my plans. Don't you think I am right, the only difficulty I see is how to get lodgings, for I could not arrive in London with three children, and no where to go to, and run the risk of not meeting with anything to suit."

"Well, Rose, I suppose you are right to wish to have your own home as soon as possible, though I shall be very sorry to lose you, but I don't see that there is any hurry for a few days. It certainly will be better for Arthur and Frank to be going on with their studies, but they are now gaining health and strength at all events, if nothing more. You certainly must not dream of going up to town on the mere chance of finding lodgings in that way; why, in the first place, you would be sure to get into some place you did not like, and could not remain in, and besides you would be ruined in coach hire—to say nothing of what people would think of Sir William's sister going about, with three children in her train, lodging hunting. Have you quite settled to take furnished lodgings ?"

"Oh I think so, for the present at all events. I scarcely know how I could manage a house, it is so different in England to the continent, and I have had so little experience in English housekeeping, and none at all in a town."

"I think if I wrote to my daughter, she might find something that would suit you; she has nothing to do, and I should think it would amuse her."

"It would be very kind indeed if she would, I think Kensington will be the best neighbourhood; it is near the grammar-school, which Mr. Western recommended me for the boys, and it is far enough out of town to have nice walks, so that Hilda would not be confined to streets only; and poor child, I am afraid she will feel the change more than her brothers, they being employed all day, wont notice the difference."

"Your speaking of Hilda," said Lady Fordyce, in rather an uncertain tone, "makes me feel that perhaps I had best at once tell you what has been on my mind for some time, and that I trust you will see as I do, and, for her sake, sacrifice your own immediate feelings." Lady Fordyce paused a minute, to Rose it seemed ten, before she came out with really what she meant. She then continued—

"You know I always have liked little Hilda since she refused in Calais to come on my lap, because she did not know me; my liking for her has only strengthened with the more I see of her sincere, natural, and affectionate ways, and I should wish to keep her, and bring her up as my own child. You know I have none of my own, or rather what is much the same thing, she is grown up and married ; I do not see much of her, and she never was, I think, fond of me in the way that one thinks an only child would cling to her mother, but that has nothing to do with this question. Do you think you could trust your child to me? it may seem hard to part from her at first, but you must remember it will be for her good, for her benefit, now and in the future. You can see her when you like, come and stay here with her whenever you like, and she will herself, 1 am sure be happy. I think she is fond of me ; you know I am fond of her, or I should not wish you to part with her to me ; and you know I will act by her and for her, as if she were my own and your brother's child."

Rose was for the moment unable to answer, thoughts one after another rushed through her mind like lightning, the fors and againsts ; however, she felt the fors were all for Hilda, the againsts all for herself. What was she to say ? what could she do ? The thought of parting with her darling child seemed so dreadful, but yet if she refused, might not Hilda live to reproach her for having so marred her future; for having through her own selfishness condemned her to poverty, when she had had the offer of a wealthy and luxurious home for her.

Rose's voice trembled as she answered, " Your proposition is so unexpected, that I scarcely know what to say ; are you sure my brother would like it ?"   She grasped hold of that idea which had suddenly struck her, as perhaps the saving of her child to herself, without doing so though for her own happiness.   She did not think he was particularly fond of Hilda, and perhaps Lady Fordyce had never mentioned the matter to him at all ; but that hope was soon dispelled by Lady Fordyce answering, " I thought it but due to Sir William to speak to him before making the proposal to you, so he is

quite aware of my wishes, and has in no way
objected to them."

"1 am afraid," said Rose, " Hilda will fret
very much at the idea of parting from me
and her brothers, and it will be a dreadful
loss to me. 1 have always looked forward
with such pleasure at the idea of knowing I
should never need to send her away from me,
that I could educate her at home; and then
again, I should fear her living with you, in
the style you do, it will give her ideas and
notions that will be hard to wean her from
when older."

"But why should she be weaned from
them?" interposed Lady Fordyce, "you do
not think if I undertake the charge of her
now, I should only be too glad to have her
with me, when she is of an age to be com-
panionable; and she will have every prospect
of marrying well. As to her fretting about
you; it will not do, if you consent to leave
her with me, to let her know it is for a con-

tinuance. It will be much better to let her think she is merely here for a few days, whilst you are getting settled, and she will soon be reconciled."

Rose felt there really was nothing to urge against it, so she said nothing, she could not trust herself to say more than, "I must think a little, Mary, my thoughts seem all entangled," and she got up from the sofa where she was sitting, and as she passed by Lady Fordyce, she took her hand, and said, "Thank you, Mary, for all your goodness," and quickly left the room.

As she was crossing the hall, she heard Hilda's voice, she called her to come to her; and she stood still till the child joined her, and taking her hand, she hurried up to her own room with her, and hastily shutting the door, she threw herself into a chair, took the child up in her arms, and kissing her, buried her face in her little neck, and sobbed violently.

"Mamma, dear, what are you so unhappy about, I shall cry too if you do," and
she put her arms round her mother, trying
with her childish endearments to soothe
her.

" My darling, I will try not to be unhappy.
I only want you to love me, and be good,
and I wont then cry."

Hilda began to think she must have been
guilty of some great misdemeanour, or her
mamma would never tell her if she were
good she would not cry. However, the tears
had relieved Rose, she felt as if after all it
was not such a dreadful thing—her child
would be so cared for, so watched, and she
could see her whenever she wished, she was
determined she would not give way again in
such a manner, besides it was due to Lady
Fordyce that she should not appear as if she
was being ill used in the matter. It seemed
hard at first, but when after sending Hilda
out of the room again to go to play, she

thought the whole thing over coolly and calmly; she knew she had cause for deep gratitude; supposing she were to die, what would become of Hilda, the boys could work their own way, but a girl, what can she do? Be a governess, she would sooner Hilda died than that; a governess' life is so dreadful, such toil and misery, and subject to insults from the mistress to servant. No, she was thankful Hilda's future was secure. So she went down again into the library, where Lady Fordyce was still sitting, and told her she was grateful for her offer, and that Hilda should remain.

"I trust you will never repent your decision, Rose, it shall not be my fault if you do. But whilst you have been out of the room, I have been writing to Matilda, to ask her to look about for some nice lodgings for you, so I hope in a day or two we shall hear of something, for she has nothing to do, and plenty of time for it."

There was a pause of some minutes; Lady Fordyce took up some netting that lay on the writing table at the side of the room, and Rose sat with her eyes fixed on the ground. Presently, the door leading from the dining-room opened, and Sir William came in, he looked out of temper, and said in a harsh tone, " Those boys have been treading down the box round the flower beds, it really is very provoking, I think you might look after them a little, and not let them be so mischievous." He looked at no one whilst he spoke, but Rose of course knew it was meant for her. None of us can bear other people to find fault with either our dogs or our children, and Rose felt very angry, though she knew her brother had cause to complain if they had done so ; so she answered on the heat of the moment, " I am very sorry my children should have done any harm to your garden, but I will take care it shall not happen again, and I will relieve you of them as soon as I possibly can arrange to do so." She rose and left the room before another word could be said.

Lady Fordyce was sorry this should have occurred, for she knew, by experience, angry words are soon spoken, but they are rarely forgotten; besides Rose was wrong, if the boys had injured the box, which was more than likely, it was annoying, for it took a long time to get it grown in that manner, and Sir William was as proud of it as of his pictures, perhaps because both were equally execrable. Yet Lady Fordyce ventured to remark that Sir William was a little sharp with his sister, that he ought to remember she had gone through so much sorrow, she was more open to take offence at what was said; but it was useless, Sir William was angry, and would not be taught what he ought to say, and what he ought not, but there was something more beyond the mere destruction done to the garden, which turned out a trifle after all, that had irritated Sir William; he had found on going, as was his custom, to pay his morning visit to the stable, his favourite mare with one of her knees broken. The groom had been sent early in the morning, into the town of Chadwick, which was the nearest to Burwood, being about two miles off. Instead of walking, he took the mare, whose foot slipped on a round stone, and she came down on both her knees; it was but a moment, for she was up in a second, and the groom walked her gently home; when he dismounted and looked at her, he saw at once the injury done, and he trembled from head to foot at the thought of his master's wrath.

When Sir William saw it, he discharged the man on the spot, but did not utter a word. Bottled rage is always the worst, it expends itself by degrees, and all who happen to come within reach, till it has worked off, suffer as if they were the culprits; and so it was, Arthur and Frank had a good share, because in jumping in and out of the little maze of box hedges, their feet did not clear them thoroughly, and so in one or two places they had left the impression of them. When Rose heard what had really put her brother out, she regretted having given way to her own temper, but wisely thought it would be useless to say so, and that the best way would be to let the matter drop altogether.

Three days after Lady Fordyce had written to her daughter, Mrs. Phillips, asking her to look for lodgings for Mrs. Chichester in the neighbourhood of Kensington, an answer came, saying, she had devoted the two days in hunting about, and had seen some in a rather quiet part of Kensington that she thought might answer; they consisted of a sitting-room and two bed-rooms, and they were to be at the rate of a pound a week. She had not of course promised to take them, but she had said the person who let them, should have an answer by return of post, and that she begged there might be no delay in it being sent. There appeared no objection to them, no reason why Rose should not decide on taking them, and she therefore requested Lady Fordyce to write and beg her daughter to secure them from the following Tuesday, which left her another week to spend at Burwood with her little Hilda. She felt relieved that now it was decided when she went, and where, and she resolved to be as cheerful as possible for the sake of those around her.

On Thursday morning Lady Fordyce received another letter from her daughter, saying she had sent to secure the apartments for Mrs. Chichester; and that if it were convenient to receive them, she and her husband proposed coming down to stay from the following Saturday till Monday. Lady Fordyce knew she must receive them, she knew perfectly well she dared not refuse

her, for fear of what she might have to
endure in consequence. She knew her daughter's temper too well to risk offending her,
and therefore she wrote and told her she
would be very happy to see·her and Captain
Phillips the day they named.

The whole of the remainder of that day, and
the next day together with the half of Saturday, that intervened previous to their arrival,
was passed by Lady Fordyce in trepidation
at what her daughter would think, and say
at the Chichesters being inmates of Burwood.
As they only stayed till Monday, and the
Chichesters did not leave till Tuesday, there
was no occasion to let her know Hilda was
to remain; she would therefore be saved the
outburst she might expect on that head.
For it had been Mrs. Phillips' wish to have
an established home at Burwood, and only
to migrate from it for visits, or an occasional
stay in London; but Lady Fordyce was only
too delighted to have got her daughter

marrried, and therefore as she fervently hoped
independent of her, not to make an effort
to adhere to that ; she put the blame therefore
on Sir William who was too little interested
either way, much to care what was arranged ;
though when his wife explained to him
that if her daughter was to have a perman-
ent home at Burwood, so must her husband,
Sir William began to be a little uneasy. He
thought Captain Phillips might interfere
with his stable or kennel, that certainly would
not suit him; so it did not require much
urging on his wife's part to make him say,
he thought it always advisable for young
people to have a house of their own ; but he
should be glad to see Matilda and her husband
as his guests as often as they liked
to come. And it had been on this understanding, that every now and then the
Phillips's wrote to say they were coming
down.

Poor Lady Fordyce was actually afraid

of her daughter, yet she was not a timid woman; but she loved peace, and she knew with her there was none—that a word spoken in jest might cause the deepest offence, a look would do it sometimes, without even the word, and then such a volley of accusations and complaints ensued, that her mother would have willingly said or done anything to have pacified her seemingly victimized daughter.

It is not to be wondered at, therefore, that she looked forward with unusual dread to this Saturday till Monday visit. She feared it was only on account of the Chichesters she was coming, only to glean what she could as to the extent Sir William meant to help them, so that if possible she might make herself out more ill-used, ill-treated and neglected on their account.

The carriage had been ordered to drive and meet them at the Chadwick station, the railway had not long been opened, for it was rather an out of the way place. Lady Fordyce and Mrs. Chichester were waiting luncheon in the breakfast-room till the carriage returned with the expected guests. The children had had their dinner and judiciously sent out of sight.

" I suppose they will be here soon," said Lady Fordyce; she wanted to say something that would enable her to bring in a slight caution for Rose, against her daughter hearing of the arrangement about Hilda; and she feared, at the same time, displaying her cowardice in regard to her; but she thought that would even be better than a scene with Mrs. Phillips. " I think you had better say nothing about Hilda, because Matilda might, without thinking, speak about her living here before her, and it is better that should be avoided."

" Certainly," answered Rose, " it would perhaps make Hilda fret unnecessarily."

They now heard the carriage driving up

under the portico, it caused a rumbling hollow sound, that you could hear in all the lower rooms. Lady Fordyce went out to meet her daughter and her husband, and presently came in with them, and introduced them to her sister-in-law.

Mrs. Phillips had a short, square built figure, she was light, I cannot call her fair, for she was very sallow; her hair, which was the only pleasing looking thing about her, was decidedly pretty, it was fair and wavy. Her face and forehead were flat, her nose was like a negress's, and her mouth large, her lips thick, her teeth rather projecting; her eyes would have been tolerable, but for their expression and the want of eye-brows and eye-lashes, which, however, she managed to supply with some black stuff she rubbed on the place where they ought to have been; it gave a horrible look to her face.

She was very well dressed, though her bonnet was rather made to fit her neck than her head. She might have been four and twenty. She pretended to be short sighted, so on entering the room, as her mother was introducing her to Rose, she took up her eye-glass, and looking at her, gave a cold acknowledgment to her own salutation.

Captain Philips followed, he swaggered in, he did not look capable of holding his arms and legs sufficiently under control to walk. He was very tall, very thin, and very conceited, but if my readers will picture to themselves Mephistopheles, I need not distress them with further details, for in him they will find the double of Captain Phillips, or Captain Phillips rather the double of him.

He, too, had the misfortune not to see well, and constantly had a round piece of glass stuck in his eye. If people really are short sighted, I think they feel the inconvenience so great, that they always have in their possession a pair of spectacles, whereas those who are so merely for their own plea-sure, merely stick a round piece of common window glass in their eye, which, as we are always told pride feels no pain, we imagine to be to them tolerably comfortable.

Captain Phillips bowed, walked up to the fire place, stood with his back to it, though no fire was there to warm him, placed his feet a yard apart, and putting a hand in each pocket of his coat, stood contemplating the table, and wondering if the cold things already on it, was all that was to be had, or whether any warm dish had been ordered to come up as soon as they arrived.

Mrs. Phillips walked up; no, she could not walk either, hers was a waddle, so she waddled up to the arm-chair, and sat down very quietly, for unless peculiarly ex-cited, she was quiet. She took off her glove, which was very tight, and let her hand hang over the arm of the chair; her hand was very white, though large and badly shaped for her size, but being white, it looked tolerably well. She turned to her mother, and said in such a monotonous tone of voice, "As usual, mamma, the train was nearly half an hour late; I do wonder the people in the country, and especially those constantly going between Chadwick and London, do not try what they can do to make it a little more punctual; it really makes one quite dread the journey."

"Yes, my dear, it is very disagreeable, and I am sure you found it very tiresome, and you are, I dare say, both hungry and tired; just ring the bell, Tom, to hurry the servants with the luncheon up. The latter part of this speech was addressed to Captain Phillips, who was only too glad to do as he was asked, so he swung himself round to the bell, pulled it, and swung himself back. As he did so, his eyes fell on Mrs. Chichester, and he thought her evidently an intruder, and determined that she required no more civility than what is generally bestowed on a poor relation.

Luncheon came up, and they all took their seats at the table. It was very seldom Sir William came in to luncheon; he professed not to be a luncheon-eater, but if ever he happened to be in the way, he managed to make such a good meal, that you could not help wondering what he would do *were* he a luncheon-eater.

Captain Phillips asked Lady Fordyce whether he might help her to some of the dish before him, and having done so, offered the same to his wife; but he turned to Mrs. Chichester, and said, " Will you have some ?"

" Not any, thank you," was the reply, though it was really what she wanted; but she could not have eaten it, had it been given her by that dreadful-looking man. He looked impudent, as well as behaving rudely.

Rose was, therefore, very glad when luncheon was over, and Lady Fordyce took her daughter up to her room, so that she could go too, and see where Hilda and the boys were, for she always dreaded some mischief with the latter, and some accident to the former.

CHAPTER VIII.

ON Monday morning, as the Phillips's were to leave by the train at one o'clock, Mrs. Phillips had determined to get a five minutes' talk with her mother before leaving, which, till then, Lady Fordyce had cleverly escaped. But immediately after breakfast, Matilda said,

"Will you come up stairs, mamma, with me, I want to ask your opinion about something I have thought of."

This was the same as saying, "You must let me speak to you alone, you shall not avoid doing so this time."

And so Lady Fordyce felt it, for she answered mildly, " Certainly, my dear ;" and as Mrs. Phillips rose, her mother got up too, and both left the room.

Hilda had not made herself at all amiable to the Phillips's, she had been wilful and tiresome the whole time they had been there, always insisting on being in the way when she was least wanted, and invariably doing all that she thought would teaze Mrs. Phillips ; consequently, whatever accident befell any of her things, Mrs. Phillips, justly, or unjustly, laid it to her charge.

The two boys, on the contrary, behaved very well, and Mrs. Phillips took a great fancy to Arthur, because he was very polite and attentive to her, always ready to run and get anything she wanted ; and she took an equal fancy to Frank, because, she said, she thought they were so much alike—both fair, both curly hair, and, I suppose, had she not thought it unnecessary, would have added, both beautiful ; for, strangely enough, Mrs.

Phillips *did* think herself so. And she acted as if she thought so; she looked at people sometimes with a very peculiar expression, as if she were allowing them to look at her for a minute, just to admire her.

As soon as Mrs. Phillips and her mother had reached the bed-room, Mrs. Phillips shut the door and sat down, evidently intending to say all she had to say then and there, for fear of not having another opportunity.

" I really am astonished, mamma, at the way you treat Mrs. Chichester; you almost behave to her as if she were the mistress of the house, and yourself the guest. You will, I am sure, repent it, for she is not a woman to let any opportunity pass of pushing herself forward. I think her a most disagreeable, unpleasing person, and as to saying she is nice-looking, why, her thin, pale face, and sharp features with that ugly cap on her head, is quite disagreeable to look at. How

you have endured her and the children all
this time, I don't know; however, you are
very fortunate to get rid of them all to-
morrow, and I hope you will not ask them
here again.   I think you did quite enough
when you went to Calais, without inviting
them.   I don't say anything about the boys,
they are well enough, but that odious little
Hilda, with her great eyes, is hateful; she
looks as if she had nothing but those in her
face, and they seem to follow one about
everywhere.   I would not live in the house
with that child for the world; besides, her
mischievous ways are dreadful."

Mrs. Phillips did not seem out of breath
though she paused; her voice was so completely of one tone that it would have sent
any one to sleep to hear her make a long
speech at any time but in the morning.

"I think you have been hasty in your
judgment, Matilda; Mrs. Chichester has appeared to me a quiet, unassuming, ladylike

woman, and, certainly, I have seen nothing to make me think I shall ever regret any attention I may have shown her, and which was due to her as my husband's sister, if not from any other kinder feeling. With regard to Hilda, I think differently of her, too. She may be troublesome and naughty, like most children are at her age, but she is warm-hearted, and firm in her likings and dislikings. I don't know what you have done to her to make her behave rudely to you, but it certainly is not her natural disposition to annoy any one."

"Well, you may choose to defend her, if you like, but I believe her to be a bad dispositioned child. It was yesterday, after church, as I was walking up the further wood with Tom, that I saw her take away a cake out of little Johnny Webb's hand, and give it to that big dog she always is with; the boy who is less than herself, could not therefore master her, began to cry very loudly, I went up to Hilda and told her she was a naughty girl, and I gave the dog a tap with my parasol, and told him to go away. She flew round at me as if I had struck her, her face turned crimson, and her eyes quite frightened me.

"'You horrid, ugly, nasty woman,' she cried, 'that bad boy took a big stone and threw at Don, and though it did not hit him, to punish him for being so wicked, I took his cake and gave it to Don to make up to him; he shall not have stones thrown at him, and you shan't hit him, you are more wicked than Johnny, for you are big, he is little, and I shall tell Auntie of you.'

"Now this is the child you think so much of. Where she could learn all the words she made use of, I cannot imagine, she must have been very badly brought up, and for your sake I shall be very glad when you have got rid of the whole of them."

Lady Fordyce had not the courage to

tell her daughter the truth, and that she had arranged for Hilda living with her altogether; she thought, too, Hilda was not so much to blame in the little scene of yesterday as Mrs. Phillips did, so she said.

" Hilda is so very fond of that dog, she has been with him ever since she was born; little William had no business to throw a stone, it might have hit Don, or far worse, Hilda herself, though I do not say she was right in taking the law into her own hands. She never mentioned the matter to me at all, or I should have explained to her, that she must not speak in that way to you, or indeed any person. I do not think you can do much with her, unless you use gentleness and kindness, then I am sure she would be yielding enough."

" Well, it may be so, but I don't think it, and it won't much matter to either of us, that is one comfort. Shall you come up to town this season, I think you should ; you let Sir William guide you in everything, and he is so selfish he does not care what you deny yourself, provided he does what he likes. You have not been to town since my marriage, and really you will lose all your friends if you don't come amongst them a little."

Lady Fordyce did not care for the London season; there was so little pleasure to her in going to parties at the time she was accustomed to go to bed at, and she was not young enough to take part in any of the ordinary amusements; but Matilda wished her mother to go for her sake, for of course she would entertain, and Matilda could take her friends to her mother's house, which would be the same almost as receiving them at her own. Then they would have an opera box, and Matilda never went to the opera now; she could not afford to pay, and friends did not seem to think of offering her a scat in theirs. So Matilda was very anxious to gain her point, and intended to appear anxious only for the sake of seeing her mother oftener, and having her near her, she added,

" I see so little of you now, mamma, and if you came to town I could be with you every day."

" I am afraid, my dear, we must not leave Burwood till we go to Scotland, we having been absent so many months ; and you know we have only been back a few weeks, that there is so much to see and to arrange, that I don't think it would be right in me to ask Sir William to go to town this year ; but you know you can always come here and stay with me, whenever you feel inclined, and we can be much more together and much more alone than if I was in London, for the bustle and confusion there is quite bewildering ; besides, I don't care for gaiety, it was different before you were married, I had a duty to perform in going out, but now there could be no cause but for my own pleasure, and really it would be none to me."

"I might have expected you would refuse, it is generally the same with all I ask, you find some good reason for not doing it. However, I suppose it must be nearly time for getting ready, unless the train is not more punctual in starting than arriving."

Matilda got up, and her mother knew she was done with, so she said, "I will go down, and see that there is something for you to take before you start."

And she left her daughter to dress, which generally occupied a long time with her, whatever it was for. But it was accomplished at last, and she went down stairs, where she found her husband busily eating; he seemed more capable of doing that, then anything else, and he did it well, which was what could be said of nothing besides that he did.

The carriage drove up to the door, and after waiting five minutes longer than they ought, to see if Sir William came in, they left their adieux for him, inwardly not sorry at missing him, for he was no favourite of Captain and Mrs. Phillips ; they wished Lady Fordyce " good bye." Matilda gave the tip of her tightly gloved hand to Mrs. Chichester, Tom bowed, shook hands with the boys, and off they went.

Hilda had not appeared, she felt they did not like her, child as she was, and she had no difficulty in finding out that she disliked them. She was very quiet and did not speak about it, she rarely expressed her feelings ; she was what would be termed a close child, she thought an immense deal and noticed everything, but said little.

It being the last day of the Chichester's stay at Burwood, there was much to arrange and settle. Rose almost wished that it had been her who had gone, that the parting with her child might be over. The days would be so long and dreary without her. She

quite dreaded what she should feel at first;
and she thought what Hilda would suffer,
she thought of the desolate feelings the child
would have the first night. She would have
to sleep alone, she would cry herself to
sleep, and how she should herself long at
her bed time to be with her, to hear her
childish voice asking God to bless them all
and take care of them, and the next morning
she would awake up to be so lonely. She had
been so accustomed to be the companion of
her brothers, that she must feel very dull at
first, but it had to be gone through, and borne
by both of them, and at all events Hilda
was spared the anticipation of her sorrow—
and anticipation is so often worse than reality.

But we must not linger over it; like every
other occurrence in life, it came and passed.
Hilda thought it was only for a few days,
that she should soon go to her mother;
her uncle was very kind, and said he would
have a new house made for Don, and

Hilda surely would wish to stop and see it, and Don in it. It was a happy thought; for her mother and brothers were no sooner out of sight, and driven out of the great gates, than Hilda rushed round to the stables where Don was generally to be found, and took him by the collar, and dragged him along by her side till she came to a very old oak-tree, that had a seat built round it; she sat on the seat, and made Don jump up by the side of her.

" Don," she said, " do you know something? well I will tell you, mamma has gone with Arthur and Frank, and left me, and I am very unhappy, I want you to love me, dear old Don; you won't leave me, will you? and Uncle William says he will have a new house made for you, and you are to sleep in it at night, and I shall come and see you in it. Look at me, Don, do you hear, Sir? turn your head round, and listen to me, if you don't I will go and leave you; there's a good dog.

Now kiss me, and we will take a run to-gether."

Lady Fordyce had been looking for Hilda, she thought some little indulgence would make her forget her mother's leaving. She found her under the oak, just as she had finished talking to Don ; so she told her she was going into Chadwick with her Uncle to look at a little Welsh pony that she thought would just do for her, and if she liked she should go with them and look at it, and that she should buy her some cloth for the maid to make her a habit. This delighted Hilda, she said,

" Oh thank you, auntie ! will the pony be all my own ? how good you are to think about it. Shall I go and get ready, and Don may come after the carriage, may he not ?"

" Yes, dear, if you like, and run in and be dressed, for the carriage will be here directly," and off she runs forgetting for the moment all her little trials, at the idea of having a pony of her own.

CHAPTER IX.

THERE is a small square in Kensington, called Edward Square; it is not much known because it lies off the road, and unless your business took you actually to the Square you would never see it, for there is nothing beyond it; I mean, there is no thoroughfare.

Following down the Kensington Road, passing Lord Holland's park on the right, you will see before you a bridge; a little way before getting up to that, is a narrow turning on the left which takes you into Edward Square. The houses in it are all small, and each has a little piece of garden in front; some of them being, however, gardens without flowers, but most of them having a square piece of grass growing in them.

In one of the centre houses, on the right hand side of the Square, were the lodgings taken for Mrs. Chichester by Mrs. Phillips. She was to occupy the upper part of the house, there being quite sufficient room for herself and two children. She was quite glad she had decided against taking the whole, for it is not the actual rent that increases the expenditure, but it is the constant little repairs that are always being wanted in a house. The doors won't shut, the windows won't open, the chimneys smoke, the tables and chairs are always being broken, the blinds will roll down as fast as you draw them up; to say nothing of breakages and the constant new wants servants are always discovering.

No, Mrs. Chichester very wisely thought, and equally wisely decided, it would be better to know at once what her actual outlay would be, and not to be daily, or, perhaps, even hourly vexed by something extra that she had never calculated on. It was thus, shortly after her return to England, she and her children went to live in Edward Square, Kensington.

It seemed very close and confined to them at first; the drawing-room ·was very neat and clean; the back room was to be their dining-room and the two rooms above were for their bed-rooms; the front one for Mrs. Chichester, the back, which had two beds in it, for Arthur and Frank.

She was anxious, as soon as possible, to get her boys to a school. She thought of the clergyman Arthur had been with when they were in Calais, and he came over to England, but she thought it would be impossible for her to manage it for them both; and Frank must go, too, she could not separate them. And so she determined, without loss of time, to go and see about the

Kensington Grammar School. Arthur was very anxious not to be losing time, he was old enough to feel the necessity of working hard to make up for the past; besides, he had another motive; he hoped, in a year or two, to be able to get some appointment that would not only relieve his mother of his expense, but that he might contribute to her comforts. He did not like the feeling that any of them were indebted to Sir William Fordyce for the increase of means; he did not like his uncle, he thought him selfish and overbearing, and he longed to be able to render his mother independent of her brother.

Frank had grown much taller and stronger of late, and perfectly able to make his own way with other boys. He was a fine, manly little fellow, but a totally different spirit from Arthur; he was all heart and feeling, and generous to a degree. He gave everything he had. He never had anything, because, the moment he had anything given to him, he was sure to meet some one who just wanted what he had—and so they got it. His mother never let him go out alone since about a week after they came to town. She sent him with a letter to the post; it was raining, so he took an umbrella with him, but he returned without it, and very wet.

"Why, Frank, have you left your umbrella at the post office? How foolish of you! You are all wet, and will take cold. Go and take your things off directly."

"No, mamma; there was a poor girl without any clothes scarcely, nothing but rags, and she looked so miserable, and cold, and wet, I was obliged to give it her, because, you know, I had my cap on, and this thick coat, and it seemed so dreadful that I should be so comfortable and not help her. She was very pleased, and ran off as hard as she could. I am not very wet, but I will go and take my things off."

His mother could say nothing to him, only she would not trust him alone till he was a better judge of how charity should be given. It was fortunate his brother was more careful and thoughtful, for his influence with Frank was sufficient, when they were together, just to keep him at the right point.

Mrs. Chichester went and saw the head-master at the Kensington Grammar School, and it was settled the two boys were to go at once and commence their studies.

Poor Rose felt very lonely the first few days; she had never been parted from all her children before, and though the boys were only away for the day, as they returned home at five every evening, she was so used to have Frank and Hilda always with her, that it seemed very desolate at first. She disliked being alone, she disliked walking alone; she preferred staying at home to doing so. She knew no one in London, and if she had, the distance to Edward Square would have been too great for any one to have thought of going to see her, still less to walk with her.

A few days after they left Burwood, she received a long letter from Lady Fordyce, with full details of all Hilda's sayings and doings. The pony was bought, and Hilda every morning had an hour's ride, with the groom to lead the pony; next week she was to hold the reins alone, and the groom walk by her side. Don was her constant companion, and fraternized famously with the pony. Lady Fordyce was looking out for a nursery governess for her, and she was to have dancing lessons from the masters in Chadwick, which would do well enough till she was a little older. She was very happy, and sent loads of kisses to mamma, Arthur, and Frank, and would come to see them soon.

The letter was a great comfort to Rose; half the worry she felt, was the fear the child might be fretting, but once assured that was not the case, she felt thankful that she had not refused Lady Fordyce's offer. Her two brothers were very sorry not to see her pretty face every morning and every evening, but they, too, knew it was for her benefit, and there was no use in adding to their mother's bad spirits, by not being cheerful and happy when they were with her. And boys never care for much beyond a fight and their marbles.

Mrs. Chichester had been about two months in Edward Square, it was the end of June, that a brougham drove up to her house, and Mrs. Phillips got out. Rose had imbibed a little of Lady Fordyce's dread of her, and thought she would only call to say something disagreeable, she felt therefore anything but at ease as Mrs. Phillips walked in.

"How do you do, Mrs. Chichester? I called to see how you liked your apartments, and if they are what you wished, for I should be sorry to have been the means of Sir William Fordyce's sister living in any place unsuited to her."

When Mrs. Phillips came in, Rose was sitting at the window with a little round table before, covered with work; she rose, and was going up to shake hands with her, but Mrs. Phillips did not intend that familiarity, so she bowed, and took a chair Rose offered her, and sat down.

"I am very satisfied indeed with these rooms, and I have to thank you for having so kindly secured them for me.   The landlady is most obliging and civil, and altogether being so near the boys' school, it is exactly what I wanted."

" Have you heard lately from Burwood?" asked Mrs. Phillips. " I understand you left your little girl there; it was clever of you to manage it so quietly and so well, but my mother is easily duped, so I suppose you had not much trouble."

"I don't quite understand you, Mrs. Phillips," answered Mrs. Chichester, "I am not aware of having left my little girl under your mother's charge, in any manner that should call forth such a remark; it was at your mother's earnest request I did so, and not by any wish of mine."

"Then why was there all that deceit practised at the time; there was no mention made of it in any way whilst I was there, only the day before you left."

"That is easily accounted for, for your mother, with her usual kindness of heart, thought it would be giving useless sorrow to my child, were she to hear beforehand she was to be left, and so it was decided nothing should be said by either of us, for fear of her hearing of it; but I think it due to Lady Fordyce that the matter should not be discussed between us. I hope Captain Phillips is quite well?"

"Yes, thank you, he is always well, though

he looks far from strong. Are your boys at home? I should like to see your youngest son's face again, it was a sweet face, one could not help liking him; he might almost pass for my brother, he is so fair; don't you think there is some resemblance?"

Mrs. Chichester looked up at Mrs. Phillips' repulsive, flat, sallow face, and then thought of Frank's; no, she could not bring herself to say she thought there was any likeness, but it would not do to make Mrs. Phillips her enemy, she must try and say something that would not offend.

"I don't think mothers are any judges of their children's faces, I am so accustomed to see Frank always before me, that I don't think I should ever trace a likeness to any one, however much to other people's eyes they might resemble. People generally think Arthur like me, but I cannot trace the least likeness, except that we are both dark. They are both at school, but they are always home by five, so I daresay they will not be very long, and I am sure they will be very pleased to see you."

"I am afraid I cannot stay, but if you will send them to see me some day, I shall be very glad. Are you going down to Burwood soon?"

"No, I cannot afford to travel, and I think it is better on Hilda's account I should not go yet, though Lady Fordyce has been very kind, and asked me to go during the boys' holidays; however, they are not for another month, so something may occur between this and then, that may enable me to go."

Mrs. Phillips went, she learnt what she wished to know, that Mrs. Chichester and her children were to be received at Burwood, and the door not closed on them, as she desired it should be. She thought poor people were never fit to go into society; they dressed so badly, their clothes were put on differently to other peoples. It seemed to her as if they always had written all over them,

" Poverty."   And why had her mother taken such a fancy to this poor widow ? she was not generally given to favour poverty any more than herself. She must go to Burwood, and try and poison her mother's good opinion of Mrs. Chichester, she must try and drive out that odious child.

What could her mother want with her ? it must be a great nuisance to have a child constantly with her, and the expense must be very great.   How much better would it be to increase her income, than waste so much on a girl, that at best ought only to expect to be educated for a governess, for the position her mother was in could warrant nothing better. It was very little that she was a baronet's daughter, and a baronet's sister, she was also a clergyman's widow, who left her without a penny, and three children to support. She had married to please herself, against her father's desire, it was right she should suffer for it, and it should not be Mrs. Phillips' fault, if she were not soon made to feel more bitterly her dependent position. · But she must be cautious, she already found she made a mistake, in speaking to her as she did, about her little girl being left at Burwood, it would not do to appear an open enemy, she must be kind to the boys, and try to be a little civil to their mother, but she would lose no time in doing all she could to place a barrier between her mother and her sister-in-law.

So she went home, and at once wrote a letter to Lady Fordyce, saying she had been to see Mrs. Chichester, and was quite prepared to be friendly and kind; but the way she met her advances were so objectionable, that she really could not continue to see her, if she greeted her in such a manner. That she talked of Burwood as if it were her home, and as if she could go and come as it suited her, and, altogether, evidently wished her to see that it was her brother's house, consequently she had a right to speak as she did.

Letters always have a certain effect, however false they may be thought; and if it is disagreeable information they contain, they are much more likely to influence the feelings of the person it is addressed to than if the news were pleasing—so it was that Lady Fordyce, on receiving her daughter's letter, had an uncomfortable feeling come over her. She knew her daughter was not inclined to like Mrs. Chichester, but still she thought she scarcely would write all she had done, were there not some slight foundation for it. Lady Fordyce could not bear that any one should make themselves free with her or her house, she was willing enough to be hospitable and courteous, but she liked be so of her own free will.

She would have liked to have written, and told Mrs. Chichester what her daughter had said, but she did not dare to do so. What

made her still more inclined to think Rose
had treated Matilda in a haughty manner,
was the total absence in the letter of any
mention of Hilda, and that she knew to be
the sorest point with Mrs. Phillips.

Lady Fordyce was not clever enough to
see through her daughter, or she would have
known from that very cause, there was no
truth in her letter; but Mrs. Phillips had well
calculated how much she might in safety
write to her mother, and she felt an allusion to
Hilda would destroy the whole. Her mother,
she was sure, was too fond of the child to
believe anything that would cause her to
wish she had never taken her. Hilda was
beginning to be a great comfort to her aunt,
she was constantly with her, and was very
fond of her, and Lady Fordyce had never
felt the same clinging feeling for her own
child as she did for Hilda. There was
something more attractive in her to her
aunt than would have been with any other

child, for she was cold, distant and almost proud in her manner to every one but herself, and she seemed with her to be a different little being, warm and affectionate beyond measure; this must be attractive to the one person so distinguished.

Sir William looked on her, as he would have done, had an addition been made in the family circle by a dog, or a new piece of furniture brought in, that he found in the way. He was not fond of Hilda, but he was glad she was there as his wife seemed pleased. He was always kind to her, but if she came into the room whilst he was reading or writing, and asked him a question, he would pat her on the head, and tell her to run away and play with the dogs.. Hilda did not like this sort of treatment, she thought her uncle must think she was fit for nothing but the stables.

However, things went on smoothly enough at Burwood. The summer passed without

Mrs. Chichester going down, and the time was drawing near for the journey to Scotland. There was much thought what it would be best to do about Hilda. Sir William said he thought she should be sent to her mother for the two months they were away; Lady Fordyce, wished to take her, she thought it would do her good, and also as she could take the governess she could go on with her studies. But at all events she was against her going to her mother, they had been recently parted; two months passed with her would make her forget the time she had been at Burwood, and there would be the same sorrow again at parting.

If she might not take her to Scotland she could leave her at Burwood. This Sir William did not like, nor did he like her going with them, for the expense of the extra servants travelling would be very great, he said. Sir William thought nothing of paying two hundred guineas for a horse that struck his fancy, but two hundred shillings for any one else he. grudged. He was a selfish man, but his wife had some influence with him, and so finding she was bent on one or the other of her own plans, he gave in to Hilda going with them.

There was another advantage in her going, that as they must pass through town, she could see her mother and brothers; it was fortunate there was that pleasure in prospect, for she had to take the first leave of Don that she had ever done since she was born. She gave many directions to the groom who had the charge of him and her pony, how they were to be treated, and went the morning of their departure to bid them both farewell; she came back to her aunt with a very gloomy face, but it soon regained its contented expression, when she reminded her who she was going to see.

It was a short but happy meeting between the mother and child—the boys thought her so grown and so improved. Her mother felt she could have no cause to fret for her, she showed in her face the signs of perfect happiness and health. There was so much to ask and to hear, but that only was interesting to themselves. Frank was so sorry there was to be so short a time, for they were to start for Scotland early the following morning ; but on their return there would be another short meeting, and that was something for her mother at all events to look forward to. After leaving Hilda at her mother's, Lady Fordyce went back to the hotel to see her daughter, who was to be there to meet her. There was very little to say on her part, but she had to listen to more accusations against Mrs. Chichester. Lady Fordyce, however, could judge better, on seeing her daughter's countenance, the feelings that actuated her in speaking so, than when she read a carefully worded letter. Mrs. Phillips had been on her guard writing, but the tongue is an unruly member, and not so easily guarded as a pen. Lady Fordyce was glad, however, that her eyes were opened, and she reproached herself very much for having allowed herself to misjudge her sister-in-law even for a moment. At nine the next morning, Sir William and Lady Fordyce, and Hilda, with the governess and servants started for the Highlands. Sir William had not found time to see his sister before leaving. She felt this slight very much, though she ought to have known him well enough by this, not to have expected him to have put himself out of the way for her ; and yet I think if his sister had been a Duchess or even a Countess, and had lived at Hammersmith instead of Kensington, he might have managed to have driven over. It is astonishing how great people succeed in making others even lengthen time to suit them if necessary, whilst poverty seems to have the misfortune of withering it up. There is an old saying that "Time was made for slaves," it seems to me it is made for the rich and influential ; at all events, they make use of other people's as well as their own, as if it were. It is alike in everything as well as time. The poor must cringe to the rich, and the rich will always trample on the poor, and make them feel that a great gulf lies between them.

CHAPTER IX.

SEVEN years have elapsed since the close of the last chapter, but few changes have taken place, beyond the effect years generally have on people. After thirty, years do not improve man or woman, but before that, they make but little change, except on the very young, and to them it is an improvement. And so we find it in Arthur, Frank, and Hilda. Arthur was now eighteen, he had left school about a year, and had, by his uncle's wish, travelled abroad during the last twelve months. Mr. Bingham, an old friend of his father's, and who had been the means of procuring him the chaplaincy at Calais, had offered to take Arthur with him through Germany, France, and Italy, at his own expense; and he left nothing undone, that could be done, to improve him in every way; for there were hopes if he attained a knowledge of German, together with the thorough knowledge he had of French, that an appointment in the Foreign Office might be obtained for him.

Arthur had just returned with Mr. Bingham, he had quite changed from the boy to the man; it is astonishing what a few months on the continent, and mixing in good society, does for an Englishman—they lose that rough, shy, ungainly manner, so common amongst young men who have been entirely brought up in England, and acquire that quiet, easy, unaffected demeanour that one invariably meets in foreigners. There is a gentleness of manner, and an apparent interest in all they hear, and are saying, that whether assumed or genuine, is nevertheless very pleasing.

Arthur, to a great extent, needed this, for there was something harsh in his manner, especially when with his own family; and he was therefore very much improved on his return to England, and seemed to have lost much of his hard ways.

Frank was to leave the Grammar-school as soon as his brother returned; he had shown a great desire for a sailor's life, but owing to his delicate health, it was thought unadvisable for him to go into the navy; that being closed to him, his next choice was the army, and Sir William Fordyce had got his name down for a commission at the Horse Guards some few months, so that there was every hope of his obtaining it soon.

He had scarcely altered in face, but had grown very much; he was taller than Arthur. He still had that gentle loving manner, that won every one's heart. Mrs. Chichester had suffered very much in health, she looked very ill, and all remains of youth were quite gone. She never had thoroughly recovered the blow her husband's death caused her, and it seemed she never would. She took no interest in anything but her children, all things else seemed irksome to her, there was an indifference in her to all, that to strangers seemed inconceivable.

But she suffered in secret, she knew she was affected by a disease that must terminate her life suddenly, and she never went out alone, without dreading she might be brought home dead ; this very knowledge gave her a nervous, anxious look that was very painful to see. She so dreaded dying before her boys should be provided for ; about Hilda she was quite happy ; she knew her to be better cared for than she had ever dreamed would have been possible.

Hilda was now thirteen years old ; she was not improved, her face had a heavy look, and her mouth had an expression about it, that might make one think she was sulky. She had been the idol of Lady Fordyce, not a wish had ever been expressed by her but that it was instantly gratified; her uncle had become fonder of her too, he had got accustomed to see her, and missed her, and asked for her if she was not present when he was at home.

He had taught her to ride, and was proud of her as his pupil, for no young lady in the county, could clear a hedge like Hilda Chichester; and her uncle made her a present every time she won the brush out hunting, which was very often. He mounted her better than any one else was, and so he expected her to do something in return.

But the time had now come when Lady Fordyce thought she ought to be sent to school; for she had a notion, and we do not wish to say it was a bad one in the light she saw it in, that a girl from thirteen to sixteen was too young and too old to go into society. The house was generally, after their return home, full in the hunting season, and Hilda had always joined in the amusements, but she thought that would not do now. She was too old to be treated as a child, too young to be treated as a woman. Therefore, in her own mind, she had determined to send her to a Mrs. Dalton, a first rate school in London, where only a few pupils were taken, and there she could have all the best masters.

Mrs. Fenton, their nearest neighbour at Burwood, had sent her daughter there, and Lady Fordyce was so struck with the improvement in her, that she had written to Mrs. Dalton and made all inquiries; there was a great barrier to get over before she could quite settle it. She knew her husband would oppose it, but she would try at once, this very day.

They were seated at a round table in the

breakfast room, dinner was just over, the servants had put on desert, and left the room; there was no time to be lost, for Hilda would come in presently.

"I think, Sir William, it would be better, instead of taking Hilda to Scotland this year, to leave her at the same school Mary Fenton is at. She is getting too old to be so much with young men, they treat her still as if she were a child of six or seven, and it is impossible to shut her up with me; and then when we come back, and have the Wetheralls, and Stanleys, and all those people, with the house constantly full, it will be so much better, till she is seventeen or eighteen, to keep her out of it."

"What has put such a very absurd notion into your head, my dear, Hilda is very well where she is; she thinks of nothing but her horse and dog, and I am sure she will learn much more harm at school, than she will ever learn here."

" I don't mean," said Lady Fordyce, " that I think she will learn or see any harm, but it will make her old, before she is much more than a child, constantly being and mixing with grown up people. She has been so little with girls of her own age that it will, I am sure, do her good, and she will lose that sedate way she has with her; she looks as if she wanted rousing, and I think nothing will do that so well as regular and continued study with young people like herself."

" You would not have said she wanted rousing, had you seen her on 'Springfly,' yesterday; why she is a different creature on horseback; it does one good to see her take him over a five-barred gate, whilst those muffs of men that go with us, are standing with their horses' reins over their arms, trying to unfasten them."

Hilda opened the door at this moment. She was dressed in a pretty pink frock, with her hair in long curls down her back; but for the eyes, we should not recognise her as the same Hilda we saw seven years ago. She is not tall, nor pretty, but she will be, her features are so well shaped. It is her face that looks heavy; and she has a sedate look that will wear off as she gets older.

" Hilda, dear, go into the library for a few minutes; you can order tea and make it for me. I will come to you presently."

Hilda walked through the other door that led to the library through the dining-room without saying a word.

" You are, I daresay, right," said Lady Fordyce, " about Hilda taking thorough delight in riding, but that surely is not the only accomplishment necessary for a young lady, unless she is being brought up to break in horses, or teach riding. I am very anxious she should have some finishing masters, which it is impossible for her to have here; and even if she could, the constant interruptions from one thing and another would prevent her having any real benefit. Miss Williams has done very well for her till now, but it is quite necessary she should have other instruction to what she can give her."

"It will be the ruin of the girl if you send her to school. I don't care what school, they are all alike. They think of nothing, and talk of nothing but lovers, and fill each other's heads with more trash than she could hear here in fifty years; and she will lose all her nerve in riding. I know, myself even, what it is to give it up for a month or two, why I can't hold a horse; and what will it be with her? A girl that can go across country as she can, can't want teaching anything."

"Well, we can try it for a quarter at all events; she can go next month when we go to Scotland, and if we find it does not improve her, why, there will not be much harm done, and she need not return."

"I suppose there is not the least use in

arguing with you. I only know now Hilda is fit for something, when she comes home from school she will be fit for nothing. Schools are the destruction of girls. But you must take your own way, I shall say no more, only don't let me hear anything further about it," said Sir William, and he got up, and walked out of the room into the hall.

Lady Fordyce was sorry her husband was vexed, but she knew it was for Hilda's good, and she never gave in on a point where she felt she was right.

She joined Hilda in the library. She found her reading, the only in-door amusement she appeared to take any pleasure in.

" I will tell you, Hilda, now, what I was talking to your uncle about when you came into the room. I am afraid it will be something that won't quite please you, dear, but it will be for your good. I wish to send you to school till you are a little older, I think it will do you so much good to be with girls of your own age; you are grown so sedate and steady-looking, Hilda, that I sometimes forget you are still but a child, and talk to you as if you were as old as Matilda. And so I think next month, when we go to Scotland, I shall make arrangements for you to go to Mrs. Dalton's, where Mary Fenton is. You will be near enough to your mamma for her to come and see you, and for you to go sometimes to see her."

Hilda listened very attentively, her great eyes fixed on her aunt's face. She saw her aunt was pained about parting with her, and that she dreaded Hilda should add to it by her own regrets; so she determined to master the rebellious tears that felt inclined to come into her eyes, and said, in almost a cheerful voice,

"I am sure, dear aunt, it must be for my good, or you would not send me from you; and I will try and learn a great deal to make up for lost time."

"And now, Hilda, I have a piece of good news for you; your uncle received a letter this morning from the Horse-Guards, telling him Frank is to get his commission immediately."

"Oh, I am so glad," said Hilda. "Dear Frank, how delighted he will be, and how handsome he will look in his uniform! What will he have to do? Will he go away?"

"I hope not," answered her aunt, "at least, not away from England. I hope his regiment may be stationed in England; but till we know what regiment he will be attached to, we cannot tell. There is your uncle walking in the garden; let us go to him. He is not quite pleased at the idea of losing his companion in his rides; so you must try and console him by telling him you are not so very averse to it as he imagined you would be."

Lady Fordyce arranged to go and stop in

town for a week, before going to Scotland, that she might see how Hilda got on, and also that Sir William might see what he could do about Arthur, for it was time he was provided for. After all, he was not such a bad brother, though he did things in a disagreeable way, and he had to be asked to do all he did, nothing ever seemed to spring from himself. He was fond of his wife and fond of Hilda, now that he had to part with her, but anything that was disagreeable to him in that way, he never let worry him, because he threw it off, as he would a tight coat that hurt him, he would not think of it, so he determined to forget Hilda's existence altogether. After much writing and talking, and daily walks to Downing Street, Sir William Fordyce at last succeeded in getting Arthur into the Foreign Office.

Arthur had just returned home, and was overjoyed with his prospects; all was not so bright with Frank, he had just been appointed to his regiment, which was ordered to sail for India in six weeks. It was a sad piece of news to them all, for what prospect was there of all ever meeting again, especially Mrs. Chichester—she seemed overwhelmed at first, but she was accustomed to grief, and equally accustomed to try and hide it for the sake of others; but it nevertheless told on her. Perhaps, had she given way to it, it would have been better for her, but concealing it as she did, it seemed to be eating her very life away.

She exerted herself to do all that she could for her boy, that everything might be comfortable for him. His uncle delayed going to Scotland another week at Lady Fordyce's suggestion, that she might help Rose if she could; she was all kindness to the poor widow. Hilda came once or twice to her mother's house to see her favourite brother; she, too, felt his going very much, for she loved him very dearly, he was always so gentle and kind to her.

"You will see what beautiful things I will send you home, Hilda, you shall look like an eastern Princess; but you won't forget me, will you darling, whether 1 send you anything or not ? and write to me very often, and tell me how you get on at school."

Promises were made and exchanged, and well fulfilled. The parting was a very sorrowful one, for it seemed almost like one without any hope of meeting. Arthur went with his brother to see the last of him, and with a " God bless you old fellow," and a grasp of the hand, the brothers parted.

CHAPTER X.

"AUNT, oh, dear aunt, such a dreadful thing has happened! what shall I do?" and Hilda sat down and burst into tears.

"My dear child what is it, what is the matter?" but it was useless for Lady Fordyce to ask, nothing but tears were the answer.

Hilda had come home for her Christmas holidays, and had gone back to her old habit of riding and driving with her uncle; she had almost forgotten six months had passed since she had been at Burwood, excepting the feeling that all appeared so much happier and brighter to her than it ever did before. Her uncle seemed as glad to have her back again as her aunt, and the joy displayed by Don, she thought it almost worth having been away to be made so much of.

But the cause of Hilda's grief must be seen to. As Lady Fordyce could get nothing out of her, she sent to enquire what had happened, she began herself to fear all kinds of dreadful things. The first thought that crossed her, was whether anything had happened to Sir William; she felt sick and trembling at the idea, she could hardly get across the hall, but that anxiety was soon relieved, for on opening the glass door that led through to the out offices and stables, she came against her husband who was coming through himself.

" What is it, Sir William, that has happened?"

" Poor Don."

"Thank God!" exclaimed poor Lady Fordyce. It was such a relief to her that she did not for the moment feel to care what could happen to Don, or any other dumb animal.

"Thank God, what for pray?" said Sir William. "Thank God for that poor beast, being crushed to death. Where is Hilda? she darted away when John told me, and I have not seen her since."

"Hilda is in the library, it was she who frightened me so; do tell me what has happened to the dog?"

"Poor Don has been killed. He has been run over by the express train, as it was going by half an hour ago, just below the bridge. The guard sent up from the Dornley station to tell me, and I sent John instantly, and he has gone to bring the poor brute back. They say he must have died instantly, it is his head crushed."

Lady Fordyce went back to the library. Hilda was standing up, watching the door, tears still streaming down her face; her aunt went up to her and put her arm round her and said,

"Hilda, dear, this is a grief to you I know, and it is very sad the poor old dog should have had such an end; but you must remember he was very old, and could not have lived long, and perhaps he would have lived to suffer from old age, and you would not like to have known that at last he must have been shot, which is generally the case with dogs that live very long."

Hilda listened, but could not be consoled, fresh tears came. Do you know, reader, what it is to lose a dog you are attached to? few have not, and therefore you can understand what our little Hilda felt. She thought, with Don's death, all her joy must die too, she never could feel pleasure in anything again; her dear old dog, her constant companion, gone, and such a horrid death; she would never see his dear soft brown eyes again, watching her with such love. Whenever Hilda was not quite happy, she went and poured all her grievances into Don's willing ear; he never was unkind or cross, a friendly wag always greeted her, she was sure, when out alone with Don, no harm could happen to her. And what should she do now?

There was nothing but crying, and it is not surprising if, at four-and-twenty, or four-and-forty, we can weep over the death of a favourite animal, that Hilda, at fourteen, should give way in the same manner.

"The poor dog must have been too deaf to have heard the train coming," said Sir William, as he came in and joined Lady Fordyce and Hilda, "and, probably, blind, too, poor old fellow."

"Oh, uncle, he could see," sobbed out Hilda, "for he always saw me coming at any distance. 1 am sure he was not blind."

"Then I suppose it was only his ears caused him to have such an end."

"Where is he?" Hilda asked.

"John has just come back, he is lying in the stable. But don't go, Hilda, to see him, the sight can only vex you more. You shall have him buried where you like," said Sir William; for Hilda made a move to the door as soon as she heard her poor dog was brought back.

"Come up stairs, dear, and take your habit off," said Lady Fordyce.

It was some time before Hilda was reconciled to her loss; she missed Don almost hourly. It threw a gloom over all her holidays, and when the day for her return to school came, she felt almost a relief that she should not be every moment reminded of Don when she was away.

Lady Fordyce was to go up to town with

her, as she had promised to stay a fortnight with her daughter, and she was also anxious to see how Mrs. Chichester was. Hilda had gone direct to school; her aunt left her there before going on to her daughter's house in Hertford Street, May Fair.

The day following her arrival, she drove to Edward Square.

Mrs. Chichester was sitting in her little drawing-room. She still wore her weeds, she never meant to leave them off. She looked very ill, but she did not complain; she never did. She thought it wrong to vex other people with her illness, and she tried to conceal, as much as possible, all she suffered. But Lady Fordyce was really fond of her sister-in-law, and, to the eyes of those who are really interested in us, it is difficult to hide the truth. But she knew Mrs. Chichester's objection to talk of herself, so she determined to find out from Arthur how his mother really was, and if there was anything he thought she wanted that she could do.

She, therefore, asked Rose to send Arthur over to her the next day, which was Sunday, as that day was his only free one, at least, during the day-time.

"I think Mrs. Chichester very ill, Matilda," said Lady Fordyce to her daughter, on her return from her visit to Edward Square.

"You are always fancying something, mamma, about that Mrs. Chichester," answered Matilda.

"No, I am sure there is no fancy this time in the matter; but she never complains, and will never tell me anything about herself, so it is really difficult to know what to do for her."

"That is the cunning way she has with her," continued Mrs. Phillips, " she knows she can take you in in that way, and she is quite clever enough to take advantage of your weakness; for it is weakness, the way you act towards all Sir William's family. You do more for that girl you have with you, than ever you did for me, who am your own child."

It might almost have been imagined, that she was not her mother's own child, so different was she in everything.

"You are very unjust, Matilda," mildly replied her mother, " very unjust; I do not remember, from your earliest infancy, ever denying you a request that it was in my power to grant, but there is little use my talking on these subjects. I never mention the Chichesters, but that I am sure you will say something harsh and uncalled for to me. I have avoided as much as possible your meeting any of them at Burwood, and you yourself told me, you had never even called on Mrs. Chichester, but once when she first came to live in London, so they cannot after all annoy you so very much."

"But they do annoy me," said Matilda,

and with that she walked out of the room. Lady Fordyce had never quite understood why Matilda was so bitter against her husband's family. She began to think there must be some sort of jealousy mixed up with her feelings, because she never spoke ill-naturedly of the boys, and when Frank went to India, she wrote him a note, and asked him to go and wish her good bye; and when he went, she gave him a very neat pretty watch as a parting gift.

There was a strange mixture in her; her temper had always been bad, but she had not appeared actually ill-natured to any one but Mrs. Chichester and Hilda, and she did not attempt to disguise her dislike to both, or her desire to make her mother think as she did.

The older Hilda grew, the stronger grew her dislike to her, and if any one spoke of her as pretty or interesting, she could not contain her indignation. Hilda irritated her too, by the perfect unconsciousness she showed of all the slights Mrs. Phillips made a point of showing her.

Arthur called about three o'clock on Sunday afternoon; neither Lady Fordyce, nor her daughter had seen him since his return, they were struck with the great improvement there was in him. His manner was haughty on first going in, but he lost it completely in a few minutes, when he found the reception he met with. He had gone there with the idea that they might perhaps treat him in a patronizing manner, and he was prepared, therefore, to be perfectly distant and cold, so as to allow of nothing of the kind.

But Lady Fordyce was too good hearted for anything of the kind, and Mrs. Phillips was too glad to see such a gentlemanly, handsome young man in her room, and that she could make dangle after her, with the excuse that he was a cousin. We are often very glad to claim relationship with those who have attractions, whether of wealth or beauty, whichever of the two may most happen to suit; in this case, beauty was certainly the only attraction, but then Mrs. Phillips required no other, and so it was that she gave her cousin a quiet, but apparently warm welcome.

" You never have been to see me, Arthur," said Matilda, " I suppose my mother being with me, was what I owe my visit to."

" Lady Fordyce requested I should call this afternoon, when she was at my mother's yesterday," was Arthur's rather cold reply.

" Yes, Arthur, I was very anxious to see you, for when I saw your mother yesterday, she looked so ill, that I have not been able to get her face out of my mind; do you think anything is wrong with her ?"

" I thought my mother very much changed when I saw her for the first time on my re- turn," replied Arthur, " but I think her better this last week or two; it is so difficult, however, to find out when anything is the matter with her, for she seems to dislike so much being asked questions about herself. I often wish poor old Davies was still living, I think she would not have minded him."

" Who was he ?" asked Mrs. Phillips.

" He was a medical man, an old Calais friend of my poor father's," answered Arthur, " and since his death, two years ago, my mother will not be persuaded to see anyone. I know he never thought her strong."

" Don't you think a little change of scene would do her good? I think if she went to the sea for a few weeks, it might make her look a little more like herself," said Lady Fordyce.

" Yes," said Arthur, " I think it would, but there are some objections."

Arthur said this in a sort of tone, which prevented Lady Fordyce asking him what they might be. There was a pause for a few moments, and then Mrs. Phillips asked her cousin if he could not return and dine with her.   He coldly declined, and rose and wished them good morning.   It was very evident to Mrs. Phillips, if she wished her cousin to be civil to her, she must be civil to his mother, and this she could not bring herself to be.

Lady Fordyce thought for some time what the objection could be that Arthur had spoken of, that would prevent his mother going to the sea.   Was it money, because she could remedy that evil, or was it that she could not go alone, perhaps if she were too ill to go alone, she might like to go to Burwood. However, she determined to go to-morrow and see what it was.

She found Mrs. Chichester, on the Monday, as she found her on the Saturday.   It was easy to discover the cause of her being unable to go to the sea; she had not the means.   So before Lady Fordyce left, she slipt a twenty pound note into her hand, and received a promise she would leave the middle or beginning of the week. Lady Fordyce tried to find out what it was she was suffering from.

"Why not tell me, Rose, it is very foolish of you to be suffering, and say nothing about it, for I am sure you are not well; you need not shake your head, because I am certain of it, and I will speak out this once, if I never do again."

"Indeed, you are wrong, I am very well, I don't feel anything but a little weak sometimes," replied Rose.

"But you look ill; now do let me send Dr. Humphrey to see you, he is such an old friend of mine, that you will feel quite at home with him, and I am certain he will put you to rights at once."

But Rose was obstinate, she would not see a doctor, she turned off the conversation by asking after her brother, and whether he would come to town soon; and then she wanted to hear all about poor Don's accident, because she must write full particulars to Mr. Western, he would be so sorry to hear it. And so it was in vain Lady Fordyce urged it, she could do no more with her, but she would try what Arthur said to it, whether he could not make her alter her mind. Arthur came home soon after his aunt had left.

His mother's face always brightened up when he came in, for he was all that was left to her now, and so she clung the more to him, and he had become much more gentle and thoughtful towards her of late, since his return to England, and since he had become independent. The bitter feeling that was always rankling within him that he was dependent on his uncle made him sharp and disagreeable at times; but now he was his own master, he worked for his own bread, and he felt he could add so much to his mother's comfort, it seemed as if suddenly their positions had changed, and he now had to protect and care for her, instead of her for him; it was a pleasing sensation to him, and he was proud of it.

When his aunt asked him why his mother could not go to the sea, he knew he could not afford to give his mother the means, and she could not go without them; besides he did not like her going alone, and how could he ask for a holiday, when he had not been more than a few weeks at his duties.

"My dear boy, you look tired," said his mother, as he came in and threw himself on the little sofa that was against the wall facing the windows, he parted his thick jet black hair off his forehead, and looked at his mother for a moment, then said,

"You look tired, dear mother, I am not, but I am anxious, very anxious."

"What about, Arthur?"

"About you, mother; you look ill and dragged, and I am sure you are ill; and I think Lady Fordyce was right in what she said yesterday, that change of scene would do you good. You have fretted at parting with Frank, and you don't let any one join you in your fretting, and I am sure it would help you; you would not fret half so much if you saw any one equally worried," said Arthur smiling.

"You are all very foolish to think so much about me, but very kind, too; but I want to tell you of your aunt's visit to me just now. She has made me promise to go out of town this week, and in her usual kind manner has given me £20 to go with, so now you see I shall have change of scene and air. But about you, I have been thinking that I could go somewhere that you could be with me, and that you could come up to town every day; I think that we might manage that, don't you think so?"

"It will shorten the time you would otherwise be able to stop if I do, mother; but I don't either like the idea of your going alone, we will talk it over this evening. The first thing to settle is where we can go."

The servant walked in, and handed a small pink note to Arthur, and said a person waited for an answer. It was such a rare thing for him to receive a letter, that his mother enquired who it was from; Arthur was still too much the boy not to feel being treated so, or as he thought like a child. He did not like being asked who his note was from, so he did not answer till he had read it and put it in his pocket, and then said,

"Mrs. Phillips; she wishes me to dine there this evening, but I shall not go."

"Oh, do go, Arthur, you will displease your aunt; and it is very kind of Mrs. Phillips to ask you."

"Displease my aunt, what has she to be displeased at in the matter?" said Arthur, his colour mounting up with anger, "and as to its being kind of Mrs. Phillips to ask me, why did she not ask you? I shall not go." He got up from the sofa, and sat down at the table in the middle of the room, took up a pen, opened the blotting book, and began writing. His mother came up to him.

"Arthur," she said, "you are no longer a child, you are a man, try and act like one; take my advice this time, and go dine at your cousin's, don't make her your enemy, my child, for she might prove a bitter one."

"No, mother, I feel I am right, I will not dine or break bread inside her house till I do so with you with me, but to please you, I will say I will go in the evening after dinner."

Arthur was hot tempered and obstinate, his mother knew she would do no more by urging it, it was better to let him act his own way than perhaps cause words between themselves, and she could not help feeling he was acting under a right and proper feeling. He went in the evening. There had been a dinner party, for there were three or four ladies in the drawing-room; the gentlemen were still down stairs, so he had been invited to fill up a vacant place, to be made use of; how glad he was he had not gone, he even regretted being there at all.

His cousin was sitting on the sofa, talking to an elderly lady. He thought it right as she was the hostess to go up to her first. He looked very handsome to-night.

" It was very unkind of you not to dine with us," said Mrs. Phillips, holding out her hand.

" My mother is so much alone," he replied, " that I never leave her when I can be with her, but from necessity." He turned round to look for his aunt, but Mrs. Phillips had not done with him yet.

" Let me introduce my cousin, Mr. Chichester to you, Lady Willesden," she said turning to the old lady by the side of her.

"Arthur, this is a very old friend of mine, and my mother's," Arthur bowed, he looked at the lady, he had an idea he had heard the name before, but he could not remember when or where; she had a charming expression in her face that attracted at once; she must have been old, more than seventy. She was beautifully dressed, dressed in a manner you seldom see old ladies dressed in now; she had on a brocaded dress that looked like herself, so stately and good was it, high up to her chin, you could see no wizzened wrinkled throat, all was hidden by something soft and white looking; the same with her arms, something was over them, you only saw a small white hand, that must have been very pretty, and it was covered with diamond and emerald rings. Her face was equally surrounded by white lace and white ribbon, her smooth braids of silver hair came over her forehead, and you now can see Lady Willesden as I saw her, a perfect specimen of an English lady. She held out her hand to Arthur, and said in such a clear voice, you could scarcely believe it came from the old lady.

"I must claim acquaintance with you through another channel, for I think you must be the son of George Chichester, the old and beloved friend of my nephew, Frank Bingham."

"I am," said Arthur, accepting her proffered hand, and taking a chair that was near the sofa, he sat down near her, "and I thought when Mrs. Phillips mentioned your name, it was not unfamiliar to me ; did you know my father ?"

"No, if you mean by knowing him, having done so personally, but I have heard so much of him, that I always felt as if he were an old friend. You have another brother, have you not, and a sister ?"

"Yes," said Arthur, "my brother Frank, who is godson to your nephew Mr. Bingham. He has just gone out to India with his regiment, and my sister Hilda, who has always, since my poor father's death, lived with my uncle and Lady Fordyce."

"And your mother?" said Lady Willesden, hesitatingly.

"My mother lives at Kensington; I live with her." Arthur fell a little into his old haughty tone, he could not tell why, had he been asked, perhaps it was the way she asked it in.

"Would your mother allow me to call on her, Mr. Chichester? It would give me much pleasure to make her acquaintance, if she will not think it an intrusion."

"My mother will be proud and happy to see you, Lady Willesden." And Arthur relapsed into the cordial tone the expression of Lady Willesden's face first impressed him with.

"I cannot let you flirt there any longer, Arthur; my sister-in-law, Miss Phillips, is very anxious to be introduced to you. She has been asking me who that dark, Spanish-looking man is. I won't tell you what else she said, for fear of your becoming conceited," said Mrs. Phillips, who waddled up to Arthur.

Mrs. Phillips had a disagreeable way of laughing all the time she was speaking, probably, to make one think her good-tempered.

Arthur rose as she spoke, but did not seem inclined to do more.

"I must, if you will allow me," said he, "speak to my aunt, as I have not yet seen her, and then I must make haste home."

"Does your mamma think you ought not to be out late?" said Mrs. Phillips, loud enough for every one to have heard it.

He felt that she meant him to be piqued into remaining; he determined, however, to go as soon as he had seen Lady Fordyce.

She was in the back drawing-room, talking to a tall, fair girl, about eighteen, who was leaning against the piano. She turned round to look at Arthur as he came up to his aunt, and showed a gentle, pretty face.

Arthur gave an involuntary sort of bow as he had to pass close by her, which she returned.

" I am glad you are come, I gave you up," said Lady Fordyce. " Come and sit down here," and she moved her dress, so as to make room for Arthur by her side.

He looked up to see if the fair face was still standing opposite to him. He could not sit if *she* were standing; but she was gone, so he sat down by his aunt.

She then told him how shocked she had been at seeing his mother so ill, and though she had promised to go out of town, she so wished Arthur could go too. If Arthur possibly could manage it.

She knew she could not tell him she was willing to bear the expenses, because he was too independent to accept her offer; but if she could only get him to promise, it would be enough, as she would make Hilda give her mother a present, to enable her to make up the difference to Arthur.

Oh, what a curse money is, or the want of it! What will we not do to obtain it? All the crimes that are committed, is not money in every case the cause? From the unfortunate girl who risks her soul's salvation, to the peer's daughter who barters her heart, what is it for?—Money.

May God forgive both!

CHAPTER XI.

Mrs. Chichester went to Westbourne for three weeks, and Arthur went with her. It did Arthur good, but there was little good to be done for Rose. Change of scene and the fresh sea breezes seemed to renovate her for the time being, but only served to show the change that had taken place in her, when she returned. She was more feeble, more incapable of doing the little duties she still thought she had to perform, and which, no doubt, gave her a kind of pleasure, as she imagined she was still useful.

When she came back to town, Hilda came to see her. She never went to see her mother at Kensington, but that an uncomfortable feeling came over her that she was better dressed than her mother, that she drove there in a carriage, and yet her mother had no carriage to drive in; that she had not a wish ungratified, yet her mother seemed to want many comforts that she had and yet did not care for.

But she could help her. Once or twice her aunt had given her ten pounds, and told her she was to give it her mother to get any little thing that was wanted for Arthur; she never let Hilda give to her brother, but Mrs. Chichester knew well what it meant, and felt the delicacy of her sister-in-law's way of acting.

"Why, Hilda, my dear child, you are nearly as tall as I am," said Mrs. Chichester, one day that Hilda went to see her, before she was returning to Burwood for the holidays.

": Well, mamma, I am fifteen and a half,

and I shall leave school this time next year."

" And I suppose you will be very glad when the time comes ?" rejoined her mother.

" No, I don't much care; I am looking to my holidays, because you and Arthur are coming to Burwood for the Christmas week; and aunt wrote and told me Uncle William has bought me such a beautiful hunter to hunt with, and there are to be lots of people staying in the house. I only hope those horrid Phillips's won't be there !"

" Why, dear, Mrs. Phillips always seems very kind to you, and Captain Phillips is so little seen at all, that it can scarcely matter whether he is there or not."

" But it does matter, because I hate him, and I know he hates me, and she is so very disagreeable; and I know my aunt does not like her, at least she likes her of course, because she is her own daughter; but she always seems afraid of speaking when she is there, and I know Uncle William can't bear her, because he says it always makes him ill to look at an ugly face, and so I am sure he must be ill the whole time she is· in the house."

"Did your aunt tell you who was to be there?"

"She told me Lady Willesden and her daughter, and her nephew, Mr. Bingham, dear Frank's godfather; but I don't know anyone else; oh yes, I think she told me that a relation of dear old Mr. Western's was coming on purpose to meet you, but I don't know his name. I am so glad you and Arthur are coming; how I wish Frank could have been with us too, then we should not have a thing to wish for."

Her mother looked at her, she could not help enjoying her young fresh feelings, a horse, her mother, and brothers, that seemed the extent of her desires; oh how long would that suffice! how long would she be able to say the same? Mrs. Chichester remembered, too, that when she had her brother at home from college, she wanted nothing more; but she remembered, too, how soon something else came, how other feelings seemed to be born in her, how everything sunk into insignificance compared with that new born sensation. She could only pray that her child might be spared what she had suffered, might never know the anguish she had. And why should she? she was so differently circumstanced, she had two mothers almost, whereas poor Rose had never known one. Would she not have her aunt's eye always on her? why then should she ever fall into sorrow, for she would be guarded from it.

The day after seeing her mother, Hilda went down to Burwood. She felt more pleased at going home this year than she had ever done before. The idea that she was no longer a child had a great charm in it, and she looked older than she was. She was greatly improving ; she was taller, as tall probably, as she ever would be ; she was of the middle height, but she was slight and graceful, which made her, when not near others, look taller than she really was. Her complexion was very clear and dark, with scarcely any colour, excepting when under any excitement, or from exercise; her mouth was peculiarly pleasing, full lips, and a bright red, and when she smiled, she showed teeth that looked like a row of pearls, they were so white and even.

Lady Fordyce felt very proud of her, she was what she wished her to be, and Hilda tried to be all she could to her aunt. They were expecting the house to be full the week before Christmas, till over the New Year. The first arrival after Mrs. Chichester and Arthur, was Lord and Lady Willesden; we know her already, he was a jovial old fashioned county gentleman—they never had travelled by railway yet, and never intended to ; they thought it quite unnecessary to risk their lives, as they imagined it was doing, when they had their own comfortable travelling carriage.

As they drove up, they looked as if they and the carriage had been made for each other, so well they fitted. It took five minutes for them to alight. Arthur was there to offer his arm, he liked old Lady Willesden, and when he liked any one, he could be so very agreeable; and she was pleased with his attention. "It is not often, my dear," she said to his mother, "that young men think it necessary to be polite to an old woman."

Hilda was anxious for something more lively to arrive; the evenings were long and stupid, Arthur had Lady Willesden, his Lord-ship and Sir William had farming conversa-tions, and Lady Fordyce and her mother talked generally of her, which was in no way interesting ; and so it was with joy she heard

Mr. Bingham and his friend were to arrive the next day. She expected to have found both young, but Mr. Bingham was what she considered an old man, he was about forty, middle height, and nothing remarkable to notice in him, but that he was a thorough gentleman.

Walter Wentworth, his friend and a connection of Mr. Western's, was young enough to have been his son. He was but twenty-three, but he looked at least three and thirty; he was very tall, very slight, but broad, square shoulders; his hair was very black, and his eyebrows were rather too black and marked; his forehead high, and his hair grew back from it at the temples; his eyes were dark deep blue, with full long black lashes; his nose was large and well-shaped; his mouth was perhaps the handsomest feature in his face, the lips were full, but it look as if it were chiselled, it was so beautifully shaped, and his teeth were large white and even. He was a man no one would see without asking who he was. The expression of his face was peculiar, you were not quite sure what his temper might be.

He walked into the drawing-room behind Mr. Bingham; no one was in the room, so they had time to look about them, and admire the walls, which were so much more worthy of admiration than any others in the house, for they were free from odious pictures, and were decorated with paper with flower and fresco water-coloured drawings on them.

"I suppose they are all out," said Mr. Bingham, "but if so they will come and tell us, and we can take a stroll, too."

"It is very cold," answered his friend, "the inside of the house is the pleasantest."

Presently the servant came in, and asked the two gentlemen if they would walk into the dining-room and take some luncheon, that Lady Fordyce had just come in, but had got so wet she was obliged to go up-stairs before seeing them. So they turned their minds to eating and drinking, instead of setting out on an uncomfortable walk, much to Mr. Wentworth's satisfaction.

Lady Fordyce soon came down, and welcomed her guests, she knew Mr. Bingham very slightly, and Mr. Wentworth not at all, but she could make any one feel at once that she welcomed them.

" Mrs Chichester will be so glad you have arrived Mr. Bingham, and Arthur, too, for I really think he would only have come to us for Christmas-day, had he not had the inducement of meeting you."

" Arthur is a fine fellow," said Mr. Bingham, " and I am delighted that our liking is mutual; is Sir William quite well?"

" Oh quite, he is, I suppose, in his element at this moment, he and my niece went out with the hounds this morning; I am anxious for them to be back, for she is riding a new horse her uncle has made her present of, and I always fear an accident, for she is so careless, and her uncle encourages her in being so."

"There is not very good hunting in this part, I believe," said Mr. Wentworth.

"No, not very near, but a few miles on the other side of Chadwick they have some very good runs, occasionally I believe, and my husband thinks nothing of riding any distance to cover, if there is a prospect of a good day's sport."

The party assembled one by one, but there was no prospect of Sir William or Hilda appearing till dinner, for they had returned sound in limb, both horses and riders, but in a most deplorable condition otherwise, mud and rain having done their usual damage.

"My dear child, what would any one say at seeing you in such a plight," said Lady Fordyce, who had been watching for her return from her own room window, and then beckoned to her to come up. You have not too much time to dress, and I want you to look nice, for Mr. Bingham has arrived, and he will expect something wonderful in the daughter of his old friend Chichester. I am afraid he will be sadly disappointed," she added smiling, and looking at her as if she thought nothing could be more perfect than her darling Hilda.

"I am so glad he has come, and is Mr. Western's cousin arrived with him?"

"Yes, they came together, but run and get dressed."

She was soon ready and ran down into the drawing-room, where she found her brother and Mr. Bingham.

"Well, Hilda, here you are at last, Mr. Bingham has been asking for you more than once."

Mr. Bingham went up to her and shook

hands, and evidently was astonished at something, for he looked so, but he said nothing.

"Are you tired, Hilda?" said her brother.

"I am rather," she replied, "we had a very long day; I wish Arthur you would come the day after to-morrow with us."

"I will, little girl, if you are very anxious about it." He stood behind her with a hand on each shoulder; he always called her little girl, when he felt proud of her, and he thought her looking peculiarly nice this evening.

"What a daring rider you are, my dear! I congratulate you on being home without your neck being broken," said old Lady Willesden, who had just come in with Lady Fordyce.

"I won't have you attempt to put down Hilda's pluck, Lady Willesden," said Sir William, who came in at the door leading from the library, in time to hear the end of her speech.

"You need not be afraid, uncle," said Hilda, "it would require the broken neck to make me know what fear is on horseback; but I am a dreadful coward, nevertheless, Lady Willesden. I often make Strange put a pair of my uncle's big shooting boots outside my room at night. So that if any thieves should come, they might think there would be a too formidable antagonist inside for them to attempt to come in."

A general laugh was against Hilda in a moment.

Mrs. Chichester and old Lord Willesden had joined the others, and Colonel and Mrs. and Miss Fenton were announced.

The Fentons were the nearest neighbours the Fordyces had. Colonel Fenton was an agreeable little man, who seemed much in awe of his wife, who, being an Honourable, thought she might give herself great airs, and had always some relationship or connection with every one whose name could be found in the Peerage. Their only daughter had been educated at the school where Hilda was. She was about four years Hilda's senior. She was not pretty, but ladylike, and had a kind, gentle disposition.

There was also an only son, who came into the drawing-room about ten minutes after they had. He was not prepossessing; he was short and square-looking, rather reddish hair, and a long face. He thought himself tall and handsome. His father and sister were afraid of him; his mother thought him charming, so like dear Lord Lauderdale, who, poor, dear man, only died last year, and for whom they were still in mourning. It was true he was only a very far-off cousin, but they had been so intimate, so much together, it was like losing a brother.

All were now assembled but Mr. Wentworth; the gong had been certainly loud enough for him to have heard it, but Sir William rung, and desired John to go up and tell him dinner was waiting. He was down in a minute, apologizing for the mistake he had made, his watch had stopped. But there was not much time for making or receiving excuses, for they all paired off, and walked into the dining-room.

Hilda, to her disgust, had to take Mr. Fenton's arm, she disliked him so very much; but there was no help for it, for Mr. Wentworth had to take Miss Fenton, and Arthur went in by himself.

At table, she had Mr. Bingham on the other side of her, so she determined to talk to him all the time. Captain Phillips was opposite to her; she had scarcely seen him yet, for her back was to the door as he came into the drawing-room. So she thought she could, before talking, take a survey of the whole table, the people, and the dresses.

She had plenty of time for her observations, for unless she talked to Mr. Fenton, it was evident she would have to hold her tongue all dinner. Mr. Bingham was so engrossed with her mother that she had not a chance to get in a word, so she made up her mind to hold her tongue.

"So, Miss Hilda, you have been at it again," said Mr. Fenton.

"At what, pray?" said Hilda, looking very cross, "I never can understand what you mean. You have so strange a mode of expressing yourself."

' "Why, you ought to understand everything now you have been to school; but I mean simply, for it is not difficult to understand as you do but the one thing, that you have been riding across country again."

"Yes, I have," and Hilda looked as if she thought it did not concern him, and that he need not trouble himself about her or what she did.

"Did you ride your new horse?"

"Yes."

"Does he suit you?"

"Yes."

"Doesn't Mrs. Dalton let you make longer answers sometimes?" said Mr. Fenton, with a disagreeable smile, which he meant to be very much the other way.

"I answer as it suits me, and I wish you would not teaze me any more with stupid questions."

"You are not amiable to-night, Miss Hilda. What has put you out?"

"I am not put out, but I don't feel inclined to talk, and I wish you would not call me Miss Hilda, for it is very disagreeable."

"Oh, very well, I will call you Hilda, if you like it better."

"No, I don't like it better, you ought to call me Miss Chichester."

Mr. Fenton here broke out into a loud

coarse laugh, which attracted most people's attention.

" Fred, you must let us all enjoy your joke," said his mother, from the other end of the table ; she never let any opportunity pass of bringing her son's talents forward, as she called them.

" Well, it is good enough to tell ; I was talking to Miss Hilda here, and she told me she disliked being called Miss Hilda, so I told her I would call her Hilda, if she liked it ; but that does not do, it is Miss Chichester she is to be called," and he again roared out a laugh.

Poor Hilda all this time felt miserable, she knew every one was looking at her, and would fancy she was pretending to be grown up ; she expected to hear her aunt tell her every moment that she ought not to be so silly, that she was only a child. She felt her colour rising with anger and vexation.

" I think my sister perfectly right," said

Arthur, in a loud decided tone. Hilda looked up, and saw Mr. Wentworth's eyes watching her; it made her feel doubly shy, but there was an expression in them that rather inclined her to think he approved. The relief of Arthur's words gave her courage, and she looked gratefully at him.

" What a foolish child," said Mrs. Fenton, " she is not old enough to dine at table," it was supposed to be in a whisper to her neighbour, but loud enough for all present to have heard it, as she intended they should. She thought her son conferred a great honour on Hilda, talking to her at all.

Hilda had, however, gained her end by this little occurrence, for Martyn Fenton did not speak to her again during dinner, and Mr. Bingham did. She was glad, however, when it was over; it was the first time she had dined when anyone had been there, and she thought Mr. Bingham and Mr. Wentworth, must think her nothing but a foolish school girl. When the ladies were all in the draw-ing-room, Hilda and Mary Fenton sat on a settee in the furthest drawing-room.

" I wish, Mary, you would ask your brother not to speak as he does to me; I know he does not mean to vex me, but I am foolish enough to let it do so."

" Indeed, Hilda, it would be no use for me to speak to him, he would only tell me to hold my tongue, and not interfere with him; but he admires you so much, that I am sure he does not mean it. Who is that gentle-man who took me into dinner ?"

" Oh, he is a cousin, or some kind of dis-tant relation to a very dear old friend of my mother's, and he came down here with Mr. Bingham, who is a friend of his, and you know Mr. Bingham is my brother Frank's godfather."

" Yes," said Mary Fenton, rather abstract-edly; " he is very handsome, but I think he is sarcastic."

" Dear me, I should never have called him handsome; he seems a kind-hearted, good man, and very gentlemanly, and I shall like him because of his kindness to Arthur, and also because he was a great friend of my father's."

" My dear Hilda, who in the world are you talking of, he told me he had never seen your brother before to-day?"

" I am talking of Mr. Bingham; and you?"

" Of Mr. Wentworth."

" What are you saying of Mr. Wentworth, Mary?" said the Honourable Mrs. Fenton, coming into the drawing-room where the two young girls were sitting, with all the airs of a duchess.

" Nothing, mamma," said Mary, feeling very much afraid of her mother, and colouring at the question.

" Nothing! I hate being answered ' nothing,' when I ask a question; it must have been something."

"Why, Mrs. Fenton, it was I who was supposed to be talking of Mr. Wentworth, whereas I was speaking of Mr. Bingham, so you see it was 'nothing,' as we were not talking of him at all."

Hilda had no fear of Mrs. Fenton, or any one else, and therefore it was that she was no favourite with Mrs. Fenton, as she thought her a forward young lady, and was always cautioning her daughter against imitating that bold Miss Chichester. She liked people to be in awe of her; it was quite right that people whose names could not be found in the Peerage should have great respect for those who could.

"Do you sing, Miss Chichester?" said a voice close behind Hilda, she started round and saw Mr. Wentworth sitting on the vacant seat on the settee between her and Mary Fenton, and he was leaning over towards her. She coloured up, without knowing why, and answered, "No, I do nothing that is in any way useful in a drawing-room."

"She does sing, and play too," said Mary Fenton, in a quiet voice.

"Who sings, and who plays?" said Sir William Fordyce, coming up to them.

"Why, Wentworth does to perfection," chimed in Mr. Bingham.

"Do you?" said Sir William, looking at him as if he were a marvel in nature. It is so difficult for a hunting man, a man who thinks of nothing but his stables and kennels, to understand how a being like himself should sit at a piano and sing; he only thought of men doing such things on the stage, he could not respect a man who could sing; but it was very evident that he was quite single in his views, for all now pressed forward to beg for a song.

Mr. Wentworth, who really did sing very beautifully, felt as most good singers do, that it is bad taste to require pressing, and so he sat down to the piano and sang a French song, one of those simple little songs that speak to the heart at once, " Le lilac blanc."

Hilda really loved music; she had never heard any good amateur singer before, and so she sat as if entranced, gazing at him, as if in wonder how such sweet thrilling tones could be produced by the human voice; but as soon as it ceased, he jumped up, and turning round to her said, " You will not refuse now, Miss Chichester. Lady Fordyce, have you influence to make your niece sing?"

" Don't ask me," she said in such a pleading tone, and looking up at him with her large lovely eyes, that at night always looked a deep blue, that he could not resist them, and did not ask again. She slipped away into the next room, it was empty for all had crowded round the piano.

She now heard Miss Fenton singing; she wondered how she could summon up courage to sing before Mr. Wentworth, there was something that rather frightened her when he was near her, and she was glad to get away.

"What are you here for, little girl?" said Arthur who came in after Mary's song to look for his sister.

"I don't know, Arthur, I think I am tired; if the Fentons were not here I wo uld slip off to bed, but I think my aunt would not like it."

Mrs. Chichester saw her two children together, so she went and sat down by them; she had been looking so well lately that Hilda thought her mother had quite recovered, and there was no need for anxiety. She was fond of her mother, but though she did not perhaps herself know it, she loved her aunt the best, and it was natural it should be so, it would have been ungrateful of her had she not.

Two days after, in the morning at breakfast, Lady Fordyce said that Mrs. Fenton had written to say she hoped some of the party would go over there to-day and see the hounds meet, as it was seldom they met· so near, and she would be very glad if they would lunch at Hawthorn Hill.

"Who means to go with Hilda and me?" said Sir William.

"Are you going to hunt again, Hilda, on that horse?" said Mrs. Chichester.

"Of course she is," said Sir William, not giving her time to answer for herself, "and don't talk stuff about that horse, it is the most splendid animal in the field, and carries her beautifully, come and see her on him; it's worth any money to see such a picture as they make."

Lady Fordyce knew she had better say nothing, that Sir William was quite determined about Hilda going, though she did not quite like the idea either.

"Well, who will go with us, Arthur will,"

said Hilda, "for he promised me, didn't you Arthur?"

"I should be very glad to go if you like," said Arthur, "does Miss Fenton hunt?"

"No, Mrs. Fenton, thinks it very unbecoming in a lady to hunt."

"There's a reflection on you, Lady Fordyce," said Mr. Bingham.

"Well, I am not quite sure that I quite like it," said Lady Fordyce, "but I have had nothing to do with it, her uncle has entirely concluded that part of her education."

"Don't talk trash, Mary, a woman who can't hunt isn't worth her salt; will you go too, Wentworth."

"If you will trust such a cockney as I am on one of your horses," said Mr. Wentworth.

"Oh yes, you shall take your choice; well are there any more volunteers? What do you say, Bingham?"

"No, thank you, I am contented to keep my bones as nature placed them, and not tempt Providence; but if the ladies go to the meet only, I shall be very happy to escort them."

"Will you drive with us Lady Willesden?" asked Lady Fordyce.

"Well, I think, my dear, I am too old for such active scenes, I will stay quietly at home and look through that new bundle of books from Mudie's that I saw in the hall as I came down. What a luxury the existence of Mudie is? I think he deserves a statue being raised in his honour."

"Yes, indeed, I think he does; but those who appreciate him most, are people like ourselves, who live in the country. Lady Willesden you must drive with us to Hawthorn Hill, you will like to see their garden, I daresay you wont care for the meet; so, Rose, you and I will go with Mr. Bingham soberly in the carriage, and leave those young people with Sir William at their head to break their neck if they like."

"What a pleasant prospect you seem to have in view for us, dear aunt," said Hilda, "you know you would break your heart if I broke my neck," she added smiling.

"Yes, my darling, I believe I should," and Lady Fordyce looked at her as if the very thought was too dreadful. But no necks were broken, or anything else, all returned safely, and quite contented with their day. Hilda came back with the brush, and therefore Sir William was in high good humour.

Lady Fordyce would not have any great dinners, or more gaiety in any way than she could help, on Hilda's account; she was still too young for it, and she feared what proved to be the result, that Hilda would not rejoice in the thought of returning to school. She had tasted, though in a very moderate degree, the pleasure of admiration; she, for the first time, began to wish herself pretty, she never thought herself so, never cared to be so, but now she did. She longed to have done with school and everything that had to do with childhood. She was at the age, that longs to be older, to escape from all that could be looked on as childish.

Her aunt, who always watched her closely, saw all this, and felt, when too late, she had done wrong in not having quite kept her in the school-room till she had done with it. But if she had wished it, Sir William would not have let her, and a girl nearly sixteen, cannot be treated as a child of six. There was no help now, and there was but a few days more before she was to go back to Mrs. Dalton's. The Willesdens had left, and Mr. Bingham, Mr. Wentworth, Mrs. Chichester, and Arthur only remained, and they were to stay to take Hilda up to town with them.

"Oh aunt, I hate going away, I don't think I shall learn more, or do any more good at school, let this be the last time of my going—a year is such an immense time to wait.

" It seems a long time to you, Hilda, but it soon passes ; look back to this time last year, it has passed quickly, has it not ?"

"Yes," said Hilda, drawing the word out very slowly, " but I wish this one were over."

"What do you want over ?" said Sir William, standing at the door and looking in.

" This year, uncle ?"

" What for, pray ?"

" Because," but Hilda hesitated a moment, and then looked at her aunt, who was watching her anxiously. Lady Fordyce knew if Hilda once told her uncle the reason, there would be an end to her going back at all ; Hilda knew this, too, and it was for that reason she stopped, and looked at her aunt. There was too much of affection there for her not to feel she would be ungrateful were she in any way to go counter to her wishes, so she turned it off with, " because I am a foolish girl, and winter is no sooner with us than I want summer, and when summer comes I want winter."

" Umph," growled Sir William, " you were not so anxious for summer when you were out with me yesterday," and away he walked.

" You are a good girl, Hilda," said her aunt, " and you know I only act for your own advantage; were 1 to do as I wish, I should not let you go back at all, but that would be sacrificing you for my own gratification.

CHAPTER XII.

LADY FORDYCE was quite right, the year passed very quickly, and Hilda once more was expected home for her Christmas holidays, but this time they were to last, for she was to bid farewell to her school altogether, as she was now coming home for good.

She was to have two rooms fitted up for herself, her bed-room, and a little boudoir next to it. Her aunt was very busy for the fortnight before her return, having them finished for her. She knew Hilda's taste so well, she thought she should not fail to please her. Her bed-room was simply but prettily furnished, the kind of room one would expect to see belonging to a young English girl. But in the boudoir, Lady Fordyce spared no expence or trouble. It was a small room, the windows looking into the garden—that view was not very pretty, but beyond, the scene was hilly, wild, and wooded.

The room was papered with white, and Lady Fordyce had managed to pick out one or two pictures that were a little better than the rest—a few she had bought herself during some of their continental tours, and hung up on the walls. The carpet was soft and thick, you could not hear anyone move on it. A pretty piano stood against the wall facing the fire-place; a small round table, with books, prints, and every description of nick-nack covering it; a writing-table in front of one of the windows, with a massive oak ink-stand, and everything to match; a pretty sofa across the room, and three or four fancy chairs; a carved oak book-case, and cabinet fitted up with endless drawers, and little cupboards, lined throughout with red velvet, and shelves filled with specimens of Dresden and Sèvres china. A beautiful clock, with other ornaments on the mantel-piece, completed the furniture of the little sitting-room.

When all was finished, Lady Fordyce walked round the rooms and thought whether there was anything else she could possibly think of to please Hilda; but it looked perfect to her eyes, and she called her husband to come and see whether he could find anything wanting:

"My dear, it seems to me that it only wants a stable to be built in the next room for Hilda to have Spitfire in, and then she won't want anything; I daresay she would be glad enough if she could have had that great dog of hers on the rug, I don't think she got over that for a long time."

"No, she was wonderfully fond of him, I never spoke about him for fear of distressing her. So you don't see anything wanting, Sir William."

"Nothing but herself, and the sooner she comes the better."

Lady Fordyce smiled, she was always glad when he appeared to show any desire for Hilda to be home. She knew at one time he did not like her living with them, but that was long ago, and now, though he would not admit it, he was almost as fond of her as his wife.

She changed the whole aspect of the house when she came back, there was life in it immediately; the heavy dreariness was exchanged for activity and cheerfulness, Hilda's voice was heard singing about the house or grounds at all hours.

She had quite lost the sedate look and

manner she had before she went to school. She came back now nearly seventeen, after four years constantly being with those of her own age. Her last year had done her perhaps more good than the three previous ones, for she had had her eyes more open to her own defects, and she tried hard to overcome them. Her anxiety was great to be able to conquer her shyness. She had felt how painful it was, and how awkward it must have made her look, and now that she was grown up, and no longer the excuse of childhood, she was determined to conquer it, and she did. There is nothing like a firm will, it surmounts every difficulty.

The Phillips' were to bring Hilda down, as they were to pass two or three weeks at Burwood this Christmas, Hilda had never told her aunt that she actually disliked Mrs. Phillips; but Lady Fordyce knew quite well it was so, and it was only from necessity that she arranged for her to escort her down.

She always rather dreaded their being together, and there was no hope of Captain Phillips being much of a peace medium between them. He followed in his wife's wake in regard to Sir William's family, those she was rude to and disliked, he treated in the same manner. It was about the only thing they did agree in, for their own household was anything but a harmonious one; they had different tastes, and different feelings, and yet they were both noted for one thing that they did resemble each other in, and that was being the plainest couple it was possible to meet. Time had not helped to improve her, she had grown coarser, and lost the only charm nature ever granted—that was youth; she was now well on the wrong side of thirty, and with youth she lost the little pleasure she seemed formerly to take in dress; but with all that she still considered herself beautiful, and that all who crossed her path envied Captain

Phillips. I am not so sure that Captain Phillips would not have been generous had it been in his power, and resigned all in favour of the first comer.

The first three weeks after Hilda's return to Burwood, did not promise to be so happy as she had anticipated, Matilda's presence threw a constrained feeling on all. Lady Fordyce feared showing too much affection to Hilda, and, on the other hand, she would not for all the Matildas in existence have let Hilda feel or think she was not quite as dear to her as ever. Sir William liked talking of his horses, and disliked smoking. Captain Phillips did not know a horse from a mule, and never had a cigar out of his mouth if he could help it; but Sir William would not allow smoking in the house, and at Christmas time it is not always the most comfortable way of spending one's days, by passing them out of doors. Sir William, besides, disliked an ugly woman, it was disagreeable to him and spoilt his appetite to see Mrs. Phillips opposite to him, with her flat face like a white negress; and he had no means of relieving himself by expressing his dislike. He could not tell his wife that her only child was so painfully ugly that it quite disagreed with him; he would not tell Hilda because he thought it would wrong and encourage her in the dislike he knew she already felt, and, after all, though it might have relieved him, it could have done no good.

But Hilda was the ˙most to be pitied, during the Phillips' visit, for she could not always control her indignation when Matilda spoke about her aunt. She did not know what it could matter to her cousin, whether her aunt was kind or unkind to her; but it invariably happened if Hilda expressed a wish, and it was gratified, that her aunt had a shower of ill-natured remarks poured upon her.

Mrs. Phillips never could be at Burwood, unless the house was to be full, and the Burwood party were always glad to gratify her, because the more there were, the less were they obliged to be constantly together. There was to be therefore, as many guests invited as there were rooms to hold them. Mrs. Chichester was not to be there this Christmas, for two reasons—the one that the Phillips' were there, and it would only have helped to make matters worse than they need be; the other, that Mrs. Chichester was not very well, and did not care to be there during so much gaiety. Arthur would not leave her, though all had been anxious for him to go down; a young man is always a welcome guest, especially when he is very handsome, and very fascinating.

Hilda was so delighted with her little boudoir, that it was rarely she was anywhere else when in the house. She felt so happy at being able to slip away from that odious

Matilda, and go where no one dare molest her; for Hilda determined her room should be her castle, and no one was admitted but by invitation, or by making a special request.

Mrs. and Miss Fenton called a day or two after the Phillips' arrived, they were in the drawing-room with Lady Fordyce and Mrs. Phillips, to ask them to dinner on the following Monday.

" We are far too large a party," said Lady Fordyce, " my daughter and her husband will be very happy to accept your invitation, but you must excuse the rest of us; and it would be impossible, too, as I have some friends coming on Saturday."

" Who have you coming ?" said Mrs. Fenton, it having been her chief reason for calling, to find out if any one was expected at Burwood, and if so, who.

" Some relations of Sir William's—Mr. and Mrs. Graham, and their son; they are coming up from Scotland to pass the winter and season in town, and are coming to us for a few days first."

" Where is Hilda, mamma ?" said Matilda, who had been talking to Mary Fenton, " I think she ought to be taught that when visitors call, it is her duty to come in, especially when it is a young friend of her own."

" Hilda does not know we are here, Mrs. Phillips, I am sure," said Mary in a quiet shy way, as if she were afraid of her mother hearing her speak.

" Hold your tongue, Mary," said Mrs. Fenton in a harsh voice.

"I am sure Hilda does not know you are here, Mary, or she would have come directly ; will you ring the bell for me, and I will send for her."

Mary got up to ring the bell, but before doing so, said, " May I go and look for her myself, Lady Fordyce ; do you think she is out in the garden, or in the house ?"

"Do, dear, go, I think you will find her in her own room; do you know the way? When you are at the top of the stairs, you turn to the left, and it is the second door opposite to you; knock, Mary," Lady Fordyce called after her, as she was crossing the hall; "she has a great idea of keeping her room quite to herself."

"My mother really ruins that girl," said Mrs. Phillips to Mrs. Fenton, as her mother was speaking to Mary Fenton. "She gives herself such airs, she is quite unbearable. What a pity it is, because a girl in her position ought to feel that she is only a dependant."

"Who is only a dependant?" said Lady Fordyce, who heard the last words; and she looked at her daughter, and then at Mrs. Fenton, in a way that made them feel they had better not say who it was, if they wished to keep on good terms with her.

Mrs. Fenton was only speaking of some

one she knows," answered Matilda, after a pause, for she gave Mrs. Fenton quite time to answer for herself. Lady Fordyce thought it best to let the matter drop. She knew who they were talking of, but it was far better that they should not admit it.

Mary Fenton made her way up-stairs, and found the room ; she knocked as she had been directed.

"Come in," said Hilda, from within, and Mary opened the door. "Oh, it's you, Mary, I am so glad to see you, have you just come ?"

"About a quarter of an hour ago, but I did not like to ask for you, till Mrs. Phillips asked where you were, and I asked your aunt if I might come and look for you ; so she told me where I should find you, and I was to be sure and knock. But what iniquities do you perpetrate here, Hilda, in this perfect little place, that mortals may not break in upon ?"

" Why, not any just yet," answered Hilda, laughing, " but the truth is, I feel it such a comfort to know I can be alone here if I like, without any one coming in if I don't like it. But I must show you all my treasures. Was it not kind of my dear, good aunt, to give me such a surprise on coming home? I found all ready, and everything I can possibly want, my bed-room is next to it, and I feel so happy at being ' monarch of all I survey' in there and here."

" Mamma came to ask you over to dinner on Monday; but only Captain and Mrs. Phillips are coming, I believe, because you have visitors arriving on Saturday."

" Yes, they are relatives of my mother's; Mr. Graham was my grandfather's second cousin, and they are coming to live for some months in London, but come here first."

"Do you expect your brother?"

" Poor mamma is not well, and wont come, and Arthur does not like leaving her; but perhaps next month they may come together, if she feels a little stronger."

"You are going to be very gay, are you not?"

"My aunt wishes to have a few parties whilst her daughter is here; but this sort of weather it is impossible to be what I call gay; and then when the spring comes, we shall be obliged to be in town, for I am to be presented."

"How I envy you," said Mary, very dolefully; "you have everything in the world you can possibly have; your aunt, who loves you more than if you were her own child; your uncle, who thinks there is not another Hilda Chichester in the world, and can't go out without you; your own mother, who is so gentle and kind, and your two brothers, that idolize you—how happy you ought to be."

"And so I am, Mary, so happy, I don't think anything could make me happier. I often wish dear Frank was at home but he writes such cheerful letters, and seems so contented with his life, that it is selfish in me to wish even that; but beyond that I have not a wish in the world. But why should you envy me, Mary? you have a father to whom you are all the world."

"Yes," said Mary, with a sigh, " papa loves me very much, I believe; but, Hilda, it grieves me sometimes so dreadfully to see how mamma and Frederick treat him. He is quite a cipher in the house, he is afraid of giving a order, for fear it should be counter-ordered by mamma immediately after; if he expresses an opinion, it is either laughed at, or sneered at by Frederick; and as far as I am myself concerned, you know how every-thing is as well as I do."

"Yes, indeed," answered Hilda, "and I often admire your power of endurance, I am afraid I could not so calmly and quietly bear what you do. You must marry, Mary," Hilda added smiling, " you are nearly twenty-one and I suppose that is not too young."

Mary coloured up, " I dont think I shall marry," she said.

Mrs. Phillips walked in, and said, " Miss Fenton, your mamma is waiting for you. I really think, Hilda, you might have had the civility to have come down."

" I will come now," said Hilda, "and, Matilda, I must tell you this is my fortress, and no entrance is obtained, but by very special requests, commencing by knocking at the door."

" Then I shall do no such thing," said Matilda very angrily, " I shall come in when I choose, and I shall certainly neither request admittance or ask to obtain it,"

" Very well," said Hilda, " then I shall be obliged to lock myself in my castle."

" You are exceedingly impertinent," said Mrs. Phillips, reddening very visibly, even through the gamboge looking skin, " you have to learn how to keep your proper place."

Hilda felt getting very angry, but for her aunt's sake she made no reply; but by a look, she spoke volumes in it, and notwithstanding Mrs. Phillips' short sightedness, I doubt whether she did not see it.

When they came into the drawing-room, Lady Fordyce in a moment saw by Hilda's face that something had annoyed her, and she determined to see what it was; and if, as she thought, Matilda was the cause, she would summon up courage enough at once to put an end to it; for as Hilda's home was at Burwood, and Matilda's was not, she could not let her annoy her any more, it should be clearly understood.

"You have been sitting too long over the fire, my dear Hilda," said her aunt.

"Walk home with us, Hilda," said Mrs. Fenton, "you will just have time before luncheon, or what will be better still, stay and lunch with us, and I will drive you home afterwards."

Hilda never particularly liked the visit to Hawthorn Hill, but her aunt added, " Do dear, it will do you good, run up and put your things on." Lady Fordyce was not sorry to get her out of the way during the afternoon, she would thus get her talk with Matilda over, and get the matter off her mind.

Hilda ran up stairs and put on her garden cloak and hat, and came down in a minute; she had lost the look of anger that was on her face when she first came down, and very pretty she looked in her hat. Mrs. Fenton was very angry with her daughter for not being pretty, she seemed to fancy it was Mary's own fault, or at least to speak to her as if she thought so.

The three went off, and left Lady Fordyce and Matilda alone, Lady Fordyce thought she could wait till after luncheon to speak to her, it would be better than beginning the moment they were gone; and after all, she was not certain that Matilda had said anything to annoy her niece. But luckily for Hilda, Mrs. Phillips was too indignant with her, not to complain instantly to her mother.

"Really, mamma, you make that girl quite insupportable, I told you what she would be. I told you how she would presume when she was old enough, and you see I am right, that she actually told me, your daughter, that unless I knocked at the door when I went to her room, she should lock it, for no one should go in without knocking." Lady Fordce wished so Matilda would vary the tone of her voice a little, it was so very difficult to understand her meaning always; and she never made any stop, all she said went on as it were in one breath, and one tone, but being fairly started off in the discussion whether she would or no, Lady Fordyce wisely determined to put an end to any further altercations between them; so she screwed up her courage to the highest point and began.

" It is well, Matilda, at once that we should clearly understand one another with regard to Hilda. You see it is impossible that there should be constant disputes going on between you and her, when you are staying here ; this is her home, and her own uncle's house, therefore she has a far greater claim to be here, than were she my niece ; but setting any right she may have altogether aside, it is Sir William's wish and mine that she should not only have her home with us, but feel it to be her home ; and I cannot and will not let any one belonging to me so treat her or so speak of her, as to let her think for one moment that her position is uncertain. She is, and will be looked on by all friends as our adopted child, and as such must she be treated by all who visit in this house. Perhaps it is foolish, her wishing to keep her rooms quite to herself ; but I am not quite sure in the end it will not be a better plan than if any one might go in and out as they would here; for if one might go in at all times, it would quite do away with the idea I had when 1 gave her that room, which was that she could read and write and go on with any amusement or study she liked without interruption."

" You will some day bitterly repent of all this folly," said Matilda, " Tom says, ' still waters run deep,' and so you will see what this quiet demure young lady will turn out."

" I don't suppose," answered Lady Fordyce, " that Tom is the first man who has made unkind remarks without a cause, but as I do not care to hear them, do not repeat them to me."

Matilda was like all the people who have the misfortune to be mean spirited, they are cowards at heart; and it only required a little sharp speaking to cow her in a moment. She had never seen her mother so quietly determined in her manner, and so she had always taken advantage of her usual pliancy of character to render her mo-

ther submissive to her will, rather than en-
tail words and ill-natured remarks.

It was very well Lady Fordyce had for
once asserted her authority, for it saved
Hilda many disagreeables. It was bad
enough as it was, for Matilda and her long
lanky husband treated her as if she were
something beneath them, but there were
no words that could be laid to their charge—
they were clever enough for that.

Lady Fordyce spoke to Hilda, too, and
urged upon her for her and her uncle's sake
to bear and forbear with Tom and Matilda,
that it would not be for long, or often; but
when they did stay there, to try and be on as
friendly terms as possible. Hilda promised
her aunt to do all in her power to improve in
her cousin's good books; and she determined,
as much as lay in her power, to keep out of
her cousin's way.

END OF VOL. I.